TESTED

AMY LE
FEUVRE

To Anne

Wishing her a
Happy Christmas
from all at
Pigeon Hill.

TESTED

OR

THE CHALLENGE
OF ADVERSITY

BY

AMY LE FEUVRE

Author of "Probable Sons," "Teddy's Button," "Andy Man,"
"Little Miss Moth," "Chats with Children," etc.

PICKERING & INGLIS
14 PATERNOSTER ROW, LONDON E.C.4
229 BOTHWELL STREET, GLASGOW, C.2

THE RED CORD LIBRARY

OF HEALTHY MORAL STORIES
FOR ALL YOUTHFUL READERS

By AMY LE FEUVRE

Tested; or, The Challenge of Adversity

Little Miss Moth

By M. L. CHARLESWORTH

Ministering Children

The Basketmaker's Shop
(A Sequel to Ministering Children)

By CHARLOTTE MURRAY

Wardlaugh; or, Workers Together

Through Grey to Gold

Muriel Malone

From School to Castle

By PANSY

A New Graft on the Family Tree

By M. E. DREWSEN

Gracie and Grant, a Highland Tale

Neddie Gardner; or, the Old House

By GRACE PETTMAN

Given in Exchange

By J. GOLDSMITH COOPER

Hope Glynne's Awakening

By SYDNEY WATSON

Wops The Waif, a Tale of Real Life

2/ net; 2/6 post paid

Made and Printed in Great Britain

CONTENTS

LIST OF ILLUSTRATIONS

CHAPTER I.

THEIR PLANS.

"You see," said Muffet, as she swung her legs disconsolately to and fro from her seat on the broad window ledge, "we're old enough to have plans of our own."

"It's easy to make plans," responded Twinkles, who was sitting on the hearth rug making buttered toast, "but shall we be allowed to carry them out?"

"There's nobody to care what we do. Who is there to stop us?"

Robin's voice was one of abject despair.

He was lying on his couch, his curly head buried well amongst his cushions. It had been one of his bad days, but he was feeling better and able to talk. Not happier. That was impossible. It was hardly a month since his sweet mother had been taken from her children. Not a long illness; a weakness of heart; and the end, suddenly, and peacefully, in her sleep. Only Robin knew the days and nights of anguish which had been his portion since. Waves of trouble seemed to have engulfed him, and his sisters, for the past few years. Their grandmother, two aunts and then their father, had all been taken from them; and to their horror they realized that their mother's pension as a naval officer's widow ceased with her death. Only a year previously, Mrs. Harcourt had met with a heavy loss, owing to the insolvency of a bank in which most of her private income had been placed. As Muffet had remarked to the lawyer when he was trying to explain to her their unfortunate position,

"It's trouble on trouble; and we aren't old enough to bear it!"

She was only twenty; a fair sweet English maiden. As she sat on the window ledge now in her black dress, with a pucker between her brows, she looked little more than a school girl; and yet she was the eldest of the four: and she and Robin must take the lead, in deciding their future lives.

They were in the schoolroom; though for a long time no lessons had been done there. All three girls had been at a good boarding school, and Twinkles had left for good shortly before her mother had died.

Poppet was only sixteen, she was still at school; but Muffet began to wonder if there was enough money to keep her there.

"Well, Aunt Connie might stop us," said Twinkles, "or Mr. Maxwell. I think he's a bit of a despot."

"Aunt Connie is in India. She won't hear about us till we have drifted into the workhouse."

Muffet's tone was lugubrious.

Robin roused himself.

"We aren't so bad as that. How much did old Maxwell say we could count on?"

"Only about £100 a year," said Muffet. "I'm afraid this house will have to go, Robin."

The boy nodded.

Had he not thought it out the previous night, when all the household had been asleep, and he had been tossing to and fro with an aching head and back? This sweet old country house, which had been such a joy to them all, must go. He remembered his first joy of possession, when he had been told that it was a gift to him from the eccentric singer. He remembered his mother's delight, when she and he went over it together. The winters had been happy in it, with the wood fires inside, and the robins and thrushes making the outside sweet with their songs. How the children had watched for the first snowdrops! And when the daffodils and crocuses shot up all over the green lawned shrubberies, every day seemed to add to the beauties of the coming spring. The summers were dreams of delight. Robin would lie in a hammock amongst the roses, when his pain was bad. The scent of them and the whiffs from the hay-fields always did him good. His mother was never far from him when he was ill; and her gentle hand and sweet merry voice were better than any doctor's tonics. How he had loved his garden! He knew every plant and flower in it, and used to call them his children when he was unwell. Then when he grew bigger, a tutor came to teach him, but his lessons were always carried on in his country home. There had been visits to the seaside, and occasionally to London. Lately they had lived very quietly, for there had been little money to spare, and anxiety for the future had brought silver threads in Mrs. Harcourt's beautiful hair.

Nothing seemed to matter to the children as long as they had their mother; she kept her troubles to herself; and only the lawyer knew what a brave and useless fight she was making, to keep her boy's home together. Now she was gone! Robin felt that life was over for him. He only wanted to crawl into his bed, and lie there waiting for death. Something the lawyer said to Muffet was still rankling bitterly in his aching heart. He was not supposed to hear it, but he did.

"It's a bad outlook for you that your brother is unable to work for you. He is like another girl—more helpless, if anything, poor boy!"

"I had better be dead than have them feel

that about me!" he repeated passionately to himself; and tossing sleepless on his bed, he strove to plan some way of relieving his sisters of the care of a helpless cripple. He was only nineteen, but the month since his mother's death had already aged him.

Now he tried to rouse himself.

"Yes," he said, "this house will have to go; but we'll try to let it. I don't want to sell it yet."

"No," said Muffet, with a grave face. "We are young and strong—most of us—and we shall make our fortunes, perhaps, and come back to live here when we are old."

Twinkles looked up from her toasting.

"That's the first hopeful thing I've heard you say; of course, we shall make our fortunes, like the heroes and heroines in Robin's stories. And now my toast is made and we'll have tea. The kettle is boiling over. Come on, Muffet. I wish one of you could get up a smile. I'm sure mother would be heartbroken if she were to look in upon us."

Robin stifled a groan, and inwardly felt ashamed of his poor spiritedness. Had not his mother always called him her plucky boy? What would she think of his pluck now? He had always taken the lead with his sisters, why should he not continue to do it?

He got up from his couch, and with the help

of his crutches seated himself at the table. When Muffet remonstrated, he conjured up a smile.

"I'm not shattered to pieces yet. I'm coming round again, and I can talk better when I'm up."

"It seems heartless to be eating buttered toast," said Twinkles, "but there is nothing to do, and we have always made it up here, and it really tastes very good, Robin. You try a piece! I suppose soon we shall have no butter to make any. Butter is always the thing you knock off if you are poor, I have heard."

Twinkles was Twinkles still. Her face was a mischievous one; she was as tall as Muffet, but not so strongly built. Muffet was good at all kinds of outside sport; she loved hockey, and golf; was a great walker, and was proud of her hard, firm muscles. Twinkles was fond of games, too; but she was fond of everything, and would find pleasure in "the dullest corner in the world," Robin would often say. Twinkles was still his special crony.

"We shall have to live in a tiny cottage somewhere, and do our own work," said Muffet. "Even then, I believe, we shall have to earn something. To divide a hundred pounds between four of us means twenty-five pounds each. How much would each of us have a week, Robin?"

"Nine shillings and sevenpence," said Robin,

promptly. He was very good at mental arithmetic.

"But that's not the way to calculate," he added, "as we shall all be together. We shall be able to count upon one pound eighteen shillings and fivepence halfpenny for our weekly expenses. Now, how much shall we want for food?"

"I've heard of people who give their servants about seven shillings board wages," said Muffet, "so if we do on that, we shall want one pound eight shillings for our food, and it will leave ten shillings and sixpence for everything else. I wonder if that will be enough. We shall want some clothes."

"Not yet," put in Twinkles, "and we're going to earn some money, and Robin will have some; so I'm sure we shall manage all right. Then we shall have some money from letting this house. That will help tremendously. Where shall we live? Not in the town. We all hate that."

"Not here," said Robin looking out of the window sorrowfully. "I couldn't live in the village, and see other people coming in and out of this."

Then Muffet looked up with a light and sparkle in her eyes.

"I've thought of something! You remember Kate, our old nurse? She left us to go into a country village. It's somewhere in Somersetshire. Don't you know she said houses and cottages were so cheap there?"

"Yes," said Twinkles, "but she went to help her sister, who kept the post office; and last year her sister died."

"But she's still there, and keeps the post office herself. She would help us. Post office people know everything. She might know of the very cottage for us."

"We'll write to her."

Twinkles dashed away from the tea table to get pen and ink, but Robin stopped her.

"It would be much better if Muffet went to see her; she could explain exactly what we want, and perhaps might see the very place for us."

"Well, what do we want?" said Twinkles; "let us think it out."

"Three bedrooms," said Muffet, decidedly. "We couldn't do with less than that."

"Oh, we must have four! Just think if we wanted to have a visitor," remonstrated Twinkles.

"Couldn't afford visitors," Robin said. "We'll say four bedrooms and two sitting-rooms."

"And a kitchen and scullery, and bathroom," said Muffet, "and a garden. I wonder how much a cottage, that size, would be?"

Their conversation was interrupted at this juncture by the entrance of a maid.

"Mr. Maxwell in the drawing room, please, and would like to see Miss Muffet."

"Ask him up here," said Muffet. "We'll give him a cup of tea. More business, I suppose."

Mr. Maxwell appeared. He was a thin, wiry man with grey hair and clean-shaven face. His manner was brisk, alert, and professional; but he was a man who always inspired his clients with confidence in himself.

"I shall be thankful for some tea," he said, seating himself at the table, after he had greeted them each in turn, "for I've had a heavy day, and only just caught the train down to you. I wonder if you have thought about selling this house, for I believe I know someone who would like to take it off your hands."

"We have just been talking about it," said Robin, "but I don't want to sell it. I shouldn't mind letting it."

"Well, that might be possible. Where will you go? It's most unfortunate that your only living relative should be abroad just now."

"Oh, Aunt Connie is no good! She has been so delicate since she has been out in India that we can't expect her to do anything. I shall take a cottage somewhere, and look after the girls myself!"

Robin's tone was a little lofty.

Mr. Maxwell smiled.

"Well, as I am your only trustee, we shall be able to settle something, I expect. Your poor mother was no business woman, but there is really so little left that there will be few complications. If you let your house, Robin, you must not count on any rent for the first year, because the dilapidations are so extensive. I warned your mother about them last year. You will have about £30 a year each."

"That is more than we thought," said Muffet, cheerfully. "We are going to take a small cottage in the country; and I think I shall make money by keeping pigs and chickens."

"You may make, or you may lose by them," said the old lawyer, shaking his head. "I would advise you to get a livelihood apart from that."

"Well, what can we do?" demanded Twinkles. "Everyone says girls can't do anything unless they're really clever, and can pass exams. Muffet is good at games, and I'm good at nothing. I hate books. Robin is the clever one. His tutor said he ought to have a university education, but mother couldn't afford it."

"Well! well! we'll see. I'll bear you in mind, and meanwhile we must not lose the chance of letting or selling this house. I wonder where you could go, if you have to turn out rather quickly?"

"To our old nurse," said Muffet, promptly. "She lives in the country, and I'm going to see her to-morrow."

"That sounds a very wise plan. If you could lodge with her for a bit, just till I try to straighten out things."

"Oh, yes," said Robin. "You needn't trouble about us. We'll write and tell you when we're settled."

Mr. Maxwell smiled.

"And what about the small girl? Isn't she still at school? I'm afraid she'll have to leave."

Muffet looked rather dismayed.

"She is only sixteen."

"And very fat and lazy," put in Twinkles. "She's a dunce. We all know it, and she knows it herself. Will she have to come away at once? This Easter?"

"If circumstances are explained to her school mistress she will understand, though as a general rule they require a term's notice."

The girls looked sober. This brought home their poverty more than anything else had done. Then Mr. Maxwell told them that an old judge who had just retired from the Indian Civil Service wanted a house for himself and family, and he thought it very likely that this one would suit him.

"He wants one within a month or six weeks,

and he wants a furnished house, so all you would have to do would be to pack up your personal belongings and walk out. If your servants would like to stay, he would be very glad to keep them. His wife is a great invalid."

"I suppose we must let him have it, but he cannot buy it," said Robin.

"We'll shelve that question for the present. I believe he would be willing to rent it."

A little business talk followed, and Mr. Maxwell took his leave.

The young people began to feel more cheerful.

"We've been sitting doing nothing," said Muffet; "and now we can begin to act. It's like waiting in the dentist's room before you go in to have your tooth out!"

"You must go down and see Kate to-morrow. We'll look out for the train. We aren't very far from Somersetshire, so you can easily do it in the day." Robin seized hold of a Bradshaw and began to study it.

Twinkles said she had better go with Muffet, but this was negatived on account of the expense.

"It really will be rather fun," she said, "living by ourselves in a cottage. I shall be the cook, and Poppet must be the housemaid. Muffet will be the gardener and outdoor man."

"And I shall be a useless log," said Robin, bitterly.

Twinkles flung her arms round his neck.

"You will be our genius!" she said. "Your brains will keep the family going! Oh, Robin, I am crammed full of ideas for you. Cheer up! Oh, do cheer up! We'll all put our shoulders to the wheel, and show Mr. Maxwell that we have grit and pluck and purpose!"

But Robin felt he could not cheer up. Never had his crippled state weighed so heavily upon him. The loss of his mother had crushed him; the loss of his home was an added blow; but the realisation that he the boy, the natural bread-winner, and guardian of women, should be the most helpless and incapacitated of the four, ate into his very soul with bitter despair.

"Oh, God," he cried that night in bed, "my heritage is almost past bearing. Help me to be brave. I seem to have lost sight of Thee in my life. Give me patient endurance. I will trust, though Thou shall slay me!"

And help, and light, and hope were already coming towards him, though he knew it not.

CHAPTER II.

ROBIN'S VOCATION.

Muffet went off at eight o'clock the next morning. She was full of hope, and said she would come home, having found the identical cottage they wanted.

Robin breakfasted in bed, so Twinkles, having nothing in hand, went out into the garden to look at the bulbs coming out of the ground, and to plan which could be carried away with them, and which must be left.

It was late February; but the morning was sunny, though cold. She was regarding a bed of tulips with a critical eye, when she heard Robin's whistle sounding from his open window. She dashed into the house and up to his room. She found him dressed, and in his easy chair by the window; but his face was aglow with pleasure and excitement.

He held out a letter to her, and his hand shook as he did so.

"Read it. My luck has come at last! It's nearly a year since mother persuaded me to make the venture."

Twinkles read the note, and fingered three five pound notes as she did so.

"There!" she exclaimed, executing a kind of war dance in front of him. "Didn't I tell you so! Didn't I say last night you were going to be our genius? Wasn't my prophetic soul right! Three cheers for our genius! Hip, hip, hurray!"

It was just about a year ago that Robin had written a story of adventure for boys, and sent it up with much trepidation to a well-known publisher. His mother had encouraged him to do it. For though he had ceased inventing stories for his sisters' benefit, Robin's active and imaginative brain expended its energy upon paper. He had written stories for years, but had never had the courage to submit them to a publisher. He had almost forgotten that his MS. had not been returned to him. Now the publisher wrote shortly but courteously, saying he was going to make use of his MS. in a magazine for boys and would be glad of others of the same style, for he thought they would suit him, and he enclosed payment in advance.

"Oh, Robin," said Twinkles sitting down, when she had worked off her excitement, "what a wonderful event? Isn't it? Doesn't it open out a delightful door to you? You will be able to keep us all by your writing. And you'll get fame for yourself. Do you remember Frank Fairleigh?—and how you loved thinking about the writer!"

"Yes—a cripple like me! It's ripping! For I feel I can roll off tales of adventure, like cotton off a reel! My brain is full of them! If I can write so as to make an income, and give you all a home, I shall be as jolly as a sandboy! And I shall feel I was given brains instead of legs!"

"Which is far and away the best to have!" said loyal Twinkles. "Everybody has legs—they're as common as dirt—but brains aren't. Certainly imaginative brains aren't! I couldn't write a story to save my life, nor could Muffet or Poppet!"

Robin took his notes back and smoothed them out with a joyous smile; then sadness crept into his eyes.

"Oh, Twinkles, if only mother had known!"

"She does. Depend upon it, she does. And to make quite sure, we'll ask God to tell her."

Twinkles had simple faith, and much common sense. She often helped her brother when he was in the region of Doubting Castle.

He leaned back in his chair with a happy sigh.

"I've been just a grumbling fool. I never thought this would come to me. I don't deserve it."

"I shall like to see Muffet's face when she hears the news," Twinkles went on. "It will be such a delicious way of earning money, Robin.

You won't feel you're wasting your time now. Do you remember how angry your tutor was when he found you scribbling? He said you were putting your talents to a bad use. What an ass he was!"

"I may write better things as I go on," said Robin, a dreamy look creeping into his eyes, for a vista was opening before him which only he saw and understood.

"A pen can do more than a sword sometimes, or a voice, Twinkles, if one is fighting for the right."

"It can bring us bread and butter, and a house, and clothes, and lead us back to this dear old house one day," said Twinkles, with conviction.

Robin said no more, but lay back amongst his cushions with a serene brow and glowing eyes. He could hardly believe in his good fortune. To come at such a time when he was in the depths of darkness, feeling he was only a cumberer of the ground, seemed to him like a direct answer from heaven.

"God gave me this broken body, but has given me the power to write. It will be more than compensation to me for my useless legs."

This was what he repeated to himself with a tumultuously happy heart.

Muffet returned home very tired about nine o'clock. She had her supper up in the school room. They all fought shy of the dining room and drawing room; they seemed to miss their mother so much more in those rooms than in their own.

Robin and Twinkles decided not to give her their good news till they had heard her story. And she was too eager to tell them what she had been doing, for them to get a word in edgeways.

"I have had the most wonderful day! Everything has gone more than well. I had a long walk from the station to get to Kate; it is over two miles, but I found her in the sweetest post office that has ever been built! It used to be a real old farm house, but was divided into two parts. Kate has one which is the post office, and her nephew, who is the postman, with his family lives in the other part, the bigger half. Of course Kate was astonished and very delighted to see me. I had a delicious lunch—an egg and bacon pastry, and some cream, and home-made jam, and a cup of tea. Kate says she finds the post office rather hard work, as she sells loaves of bread, and sweets, and postcards, and sometimes fish and fruit when the hawkers come by, so it is a shop and post office in one. There is only one other shop in the village and that sells everything but bread. The post office is at the top of the village street; it has a field opposite and a fir wood just beyond it, and behind that is a bracken covered hill which goes up to a lovely bit of Exmoor."

"Why are you describing it so? Do get on," said Twinkles.

Muffet nodded knowingly.

"Ah, you wait a bit! Well, I asked her if she knew of a cottage for us, and whether she could take us as lodgers till we looked about. And at first she shook her head, and told me she had only one room to spare. And then she looked at me with a start and said,

"'Why, Miss Muffet, I wonder! I have been so put about lately that I seem to have no head; the fact is, my nephew won't be postman no longer; and I shall miss him terrible. He and his family are going right out to Canada, but if he leaves nex' door I wonder now if it would suit you for a bit? 'Tis only quite a poor man's dwelling, but there be largish bed rooms up-stairs, three of them, and an attic for lumber in the roof. And if you were to come close to me I could look after you a bit.' Of course I was most excited, and she got a small girl who lives with her to mind the shop and she took me in to see her nephew's house. He is going away in a fortnight's time. The rent of it is only £15 a year. It has a small kind of best parlour, and a little lobby, and broad oak stairs—real oak they are. And the bed rooms are nice, airy ones, though rather low in the roof, but the kitchen is a lovely one! It has a broad open fireplace, and a huge dresser which would be a fixture, and two cupboards in the wall, and two windows. There's a kind of dairy, and out-houses at the back; then a vegetable garden, and a real apple orchard beyond. Of course, there's no bath room, but if you think we could afford £15 a year, I say let us take it!"

Robin held up the three five pound notes he had just received.

"The rent for the first year!" he cried. "My first earnings. We are meant to have the house. Go on and tell us more about it."

But Muffet stared at him with open eyes, and she had to be enlightened. When she heard the news she was so astounded that she could not pursue her story.

"Why, Cock Robin," she said, "you're a made man! What a wonderful day this will be to us. We shall never forget it. And yesterday we were all so miserable. I came home just now thinking I would be the bread-winner; now I find it will be Robin. Still we must all do our part, and I can tell you I'm chock full of plans!"

"Go on and tell us about the house," demanded Twinkles; "will it really be big enough for us?"

"We will make it big enough. It belongs to a farmer called Cobden. I went to see him, and

ROBIN HELD UP THREE FIVE-POUND NOTES. "THE RENT FOR THE FIRST YEAR," HE CRIED (Page 29)

he said he would let us be yearly tenants, and he would paper and whitewash it before we take it. Then I asked Kate's nephew if he was going to take his furniture away. He said he was going to have a sale, so I jotted down on paper the things I thought we might like to buy, if we could get them cheap. It will save moving our furniture from here. But we must take our beds; I didn't like the looks of theirs at all. There's a big table in the kitchen I'm sure we should like, and an old oak chest, and some wooden arm chairs and a settle, and three chests of drawers, and a few other bits of bed-room furniture. And how do you think you would like the best parlour turned into your bed-room, Robin? You would never have to go upstairs then, and they always tire you so! I planned it all out; and there's a tiny strip of garden in front where we can grow flowers. Now I must tell you, I saw a card in the window, 'Teas for cyclists,' and Kate said a good many visitors came through the village in the summer, for there is a famous well and an old ruin about a mile away, and her nephew's wife has a good trade in the summer for teas. Of course, we will keep the card up and continue the teas, so you see I have not only found a cottage but a livelihood!"

Twinkles clapped her hands softly.

"It really is too good to be true. I long to

see it. Does Kate think we can manage without a servant?"

"She says a woman could come in and do the rough work. I may be rather busy in the morning and evening."

Muffet looked so mysterious, that her brother and sister saw that there was more to come.

"You see," she said, "Kate is in a way about losing her postman. Now, do you remember at Cawdon where we lodged once, there was a post-woman who used to come round with the letters? I reminded Kate of it, and said that I would be post-woman if I could be paid. I told her I was a splendid walker and could weather any storms. She was horrified at first, but I told her I had to earn my living, and though she told me it was only about eight shillings a week, I said that wasn't to be sneezed at. She did not know anyone else in the village who particularly wanted the job, for if she did I would not have offered to do it—it would only make them hate me. And I made her promise to write about me to the postmaster in the nearest town who runs all the local post offices. So you see work is dropping into our hands."

"What else did you do? You make me gasp!" said Twinkles.

"Not much more. Oh, Robin, you'll love the kitchen!"

"And we started with two sitting rooms besides it," said Robin with a chuckle.

"Yes, but we can't have everything, and a farm kitchen is so much nicer than any drawing room. We'll have scarlet serge curtains to the windows to make it look cosy in winter,"

"But summer is coming. Cream muslin," corrected Twinkles.

"And we'll always have honey and homemade bread, and cold ham for tea," said Muffet, "with a jug of roses on the table, and copper pans shining on the walls."

"And a tabby cat washing her face," said Twinkles, "and two rosy-faced country damsels will be sitting down in lilac sprigged cotton gowns, and a picturesque refined youth with genius stamped upon his brow will be reclining on a chintz couch by the open window."

"And honeysuckle and roses will be tapping at the casement panes," went on Muffet; "and strangers looking in will say, "What a sweet rural scene! A picture worthy of an artist's brush!"

Then both girls laughed together; the first genuine laugh that had sounded in that house since their mother's death. They checked themselves at once with shamed looks, but Robin's eyes were shining with gladness.

"Oh," he said, "God is good to us!"

It was not said priggishly, but was just the

outburst of a full heart, and somehow or other Twinkles felt the tears rise to her eyes as she looked at him. They talked more soberly together after that, and when they separated for the night, they took to bed with them a vivid impression of that thatched post office in Somersetshire. The next day Muffet wrote a long letter to Mr. Maxwell.

"You see," she explained, "we are minors, so we can't quite act as we like, without getting his permission. But he'll be only too glad to get rid of the responsibility of us."

Mr. Maxwell did not prove at first so easy to manage as they had hoped. He insisted upon going into Somersetshire himself, and interviewing Kate, and the owner of the cottage. Then he told them they had not sufficient ready money to buy any more furniture, and must pick out what they needed from their own house.

"It will be an experiment," he said; "but Kate seems a very active, practical body, and I shall hold her responsible for your welfare. She is to write to me if anything goes wrong."

"One would think we were still in the nursery!" scoffed Twinkles.

"You have none of you any idea of the value of money," said the lawyer. "You will find yourselves penniless, and in debt before you know where you are."

"That we shall not be," said Robin proudly. "It will be my business to prevent that."

"Robin is going to be an author," said Twinkles in a little burst of confidence. "He has had one story accepted, and more ordered. We shall be coming back here before long."

"We shall certainly never run into debt," Muffet declared. "I am going to earn money as well as Robin."

"It won't do you any harm to try it for a time," said Mr. Maxwell, looking at them musingly. "If hope and energy and confidence will bring you an income, you have plenty of that amongst you; but literature, Robin, is a very poor profession, except to the favoured few. It won't bring much grist to the mill, my boy!" Then having tried, as Muffet expressed it, "to damp their fire out," he departed, and left them to arrange things as they liked. A week later, Muffet heard from Kate, that she had been accepted as post-woman, on a month's trial.

And Muffet immediately began to make preparations for her role as such. She ferreted out a fishing costume of hers, which she had worn when salmon fishing with her uncle for a month in Scotland. The waders, Twinkles begged her not to take; but the oilskin coat and cap were packed at the bottom of her trunk, as well as stout nailed boots.

"I shall be out in all weathers, and I have a

six-mile round twice a day. It will keep me nice and thin.''

''You might use Robin's motor if you have very heavy parcels,'' suggested Twinkles, ''but Robin said he did not know whether he should take it.''

It was a present from his Aunt Connie's husband, Captain Ferguson, before he went to India. It was a very small motor with a seat for two. Robin understood the mechanism of it, and could drive himself about; but was not strong enough to clean it. That was done by the under gardener.

''Of course you must take your motor,'' said Muffet. ''How can you get on without it? You could never get about anywhere.''

''I don't expect we shall be able to afford the petrol, and I shall be so busy writing, that I shall not want to go out. Besides, I shall have no one to keep it clean.''

''I'll do that,'' said Muffet promptly. ''I shall learn from Harris how to do it before we leave. Of course we must take it. It isn't like a horse. If we do run out of petrol, it won't spoil by keeping.''

For the next few weeks they were so busy packing up, and arranging what they should take with them, and what they should leave behind, that they had no time to be miserable.

And whenever Robin got a chance, he began

to scribble for all he was worth. It did him good, for it lifted him clean out of his surroundings,—a necessarily sad atmosphere.

The Indian judge took the house for a term of five years. And most of their servants agreed to stay on with the newcomers. Muffet paid several visits to the cottage; and was impatient with the slow progress of the painters and paperers. But at last it was finished and ready for occupation, and then the two girls went on in advance with a van load of furniture to get it all ready before Robin came.

If the boy chafed at this wise but inevitable arrangement, he concealed it as best he could. Years had taught him patient resignation; and the knowledge that now he could help his sisters pecuniarily took away the sting of his helplessness in the move. He was not sorry to spend the last day alone in his old home. None of them loved it quite as much as he did. It had been his since his childhood; the giver had long since passed away; and now the old house was once more going to change owners. Yet Robin's thoughts were not bitter ones. He wandered round the gardens in the dusk; but his eyes saw beyond the house with its picturesque, well-ordered grounds. They gazed upwards into the Unseen world, which was always so real to him, and he saw there "a building of God, a house not made with hands eternal in the heavens."

"If I don't come back to you," he whispered, gazing up at the old stone porch, before he went in to bed, "I shall have had some lovely years that can never be taken away from me and I have some better times in front. I won't quarrel with life."

CHAPTER III.

THEIR MOVE.

It was towards the end of a blustering stormy day in March that Robin arrived at his new home.

Muffet had met him at the station in a musty old car, the only vehicle that the village possessed, for travellers and their luggage. Robin was tired with his journey, and his back was aching, but his eyes and smile were bright.

"I do hope you'll like it," Muffet kept saying in a kind of nervous way. "Twinkles and I have done our best. Don't look out, for the country is looking hideous in this wind and rain. Shut your eyes till we stop. I want you to see nothing but our thatched cottage, and you'll see the country another day, when the sun is shining."

So Robin did as he was told. He was so tired that it was a relief to him to close his eyes; and it did not seem so very long before the car stopped, and Twinkles' face appeared at the window. There was a gust of rain and wind as Robin was helped out, and up a little cobble path to a roomy old-fashioned porch, and then in another moment Twinkles had flung open a door, with the air of a triumphant showman.

The old kitchen really did look very nice, and Muffet and Twinkles deserved credit for the way in which they had worked; for, except for the help of a woman to clean for one day, they had done it all themselves. Chintz curtains were in the windows, and on the broad tiles were one or two pots of hyacinths and daffodils in bloom. There was a bright fire burning, and Robin's couch was drawn up on one side of it, with a screen protecting it from draughts. There was a table in the middle of the room, spread for a meal. The dresser was full of china, but the top shelf held some of Robin's books. Pictures on the whitewashed walls, thick rugs under foot, and one or two wicker lounge chairs made it a very cozy, comfortable sitting room. One of the fixed cupboards in the wall had been turned into a book case, and the doors of it taken away. On the mantelpiece were brass candlesticks and some quaint bits of china, reminders of the old schoolroom at home.

Robin with bright and eager eyes, stood leaning upon his crutches, gazing at everything round him.

"It's stunning!" he said. Then Muffet pushed open a door on the other side of the passage.

"And this is your bed-room," she said.

It was almost a *fac simile* of his room at

home, only much smaller, but Robin was more than content. His luggage was brought in; and then, when he was comfortably established on his couch, tea began.

"We've arranged," said Muffet, "to have only three meals a day, because we're so poor. We're going to have breakfast at nine o'clock. I shall have a cup of tea very early before I start on my postman's rounds, but I shall have breakfast when I come back. Then we shall have our biggest meal at one o'clock, and tea at five. Then you shall have a cup of bread and milk before you go to bed. And that's all."

"Why should I be pampered with bread and milk?" questioned Robin.

"Because you always have it to make you sleep. We went without meat in the middle of the day, to have a good meal now. And Kate killed one of her own chickens, and cooked it, and brought it in. We paid her two shillings for it, which is dirt cheap, but she wouldn't take any more."

There certainly was no stint about this first evening's meal. Roast chicken and boiled potatoes, some stewed apples and a junket, and hot coffee, proved most appetising; though at first Robin felt too tired to be hungry.

Twinkles refused to let him get up from his couch, and brought him his food, and placed it on his little invalid's table. She and Muffet were in the best of spirits, though they both looked a little tired.

The rain slashed against the window panes, but Muffet closed the shutters, and lighted the lamp; then Twinkles cleared away the tea things and washed up in the little back kitchen. Muffet put the big kettle on the fire again.

"We always have this on," she said. "I had no idea that such a lot of hot water is wanted all day long. I'm so glad we have a tap of cold water in the scullery. Most people have to go outside to get their water from wells, Kate says."

In a short time the girls had got the room tidy, and pulled up their chairs over the fire.

"It is really very jolly having no servants," said Twinkles, "but I shall be glad when Poppet comes back, because she'll be able to help. She's coming to-morrow, Robin."

"And I'll help, too," said Robin, manfully, "after I've got over the journey. I can chop wood, and keep the kettle boiling, and do some of the gardening."

"We mean to make Poppet do some of that, under me," said Muffet.

Then they were interrupted by a knock at the door, and in came Kate to say "good evening" to "Master Robin." She was beaming all over with pleasure at having her old nurslings so close to her, and more or less under her charge.

She had arranged that for a shilling a week her little maid should come in for two hours every morning to do the rough work in the house. "And though I can't bear to see you all so low down, yet I will say from the time I had you in the nursery, I taught you all to be useful and to help yourselves, and I don't see why you shouldn't be happy here. And if things don't go right I'll come in and straighten them out for you; and if Miss Twinkles will now and again help me in the office, I'll slip in and do a bit of cooking for you for just the exchange."

"And by and by, Kate," said Robin proudly, "I shall be rolling in money, for I'm going to be an author."

Kate looked at him admiringly.

"You always had a spirit beyond your strength," she said.

Robin went early to bed, and had a good night, though he woke early in the morning. He heard Muffet creep out of the house at six o'clock. There was a stir of life beginning already in the village street. The clattering of milk pails, lowing of cattle, and the crowing and clucking of cocks and hens amused and interested him. Then he heard men's voices discussing weather and the crops, as they gossiped outside the post-office. He pulled up his blind, and bright sunshine streamed into his room. When

Twinkles came with a small can of hot water to his door, she found him up and nearly dressed.

"Did you find it rather cramped for your bath?" she enquired with some anxiety.

"Now look here," said Robin, "don't you begin trying to coddle me. If you can rough it, so can I. If I had to bathe in a brook at the bottom of the garden I'd do it. I'm starving. Shall I help to get the breakfast ready?"

"It's done, and I'm going to boil some eggs, one for each of us. Muffet says we shan't be able to have eggs every morning."

Twinkles and Robin were in very good spirits as they began their breakfast together. Muffet came in about a quarter past nine. Her cheeks were glowing from her walk, and she declared herself quite ravenous.

As she ate, she talked, for she had much to tell them.

"I love my rounds. I can tell you, Robin, about all the people who live here. I heard about them from Kate, but I have been to their houses this morning. I first went to the Rectory, such a nice old house, with a rhododendron drive, and the grounds are kept exquisitely neat. The rector's name is Handley, and he has one little boy about eight, who is the apple of his eye. They were all in bed when I called—a neat little maid-servant took in the letters. Mrs. Handley trains girls for service, and Kate says she mothers the whole parish. I went across the fields then, to two farms, and then I went to the Manor. Mr. Blair is the squire, and his wife is a very fashionable young woman, isn't she, Twinkles? We saw her in church. She has some tiny children. She has a red face and a loud voice. The Manor reminds me a little of home, Robin; it is covered with roses, and the gardens round it are old-fashioned and pretty. Lady Eleanor Blair, the squire's mother, lives in the Dower house. I went on there afterwards. It is a sweet spot. A low grey house with mossy roof, and with walls filled with ferns, and lichen and stone-crop. And when I went up the broad stone steps to the door, who should be standing outside but Lady Eleanor herself! Her face is just like one in a picture; she had a big straw hat on, and was looking dreamily over her garden when I came up the steps. I felt quite shy, and though she must have been surprised to see me, she did not show it in the least.

"'I have taken John Triggs' place as postman,' I explained. 'Kate Triggs has recommended me. I've come to live next door to her.'

"She smiled then, and I quite lost my heart to her. I'm sure she is much more fitted to live at the Manor than that loud-voiced daughter-in-law of hers. She took the letters from me.

" 'I am a bad sleeper,' she said, 'so I come out into the garden in the sweetest time of day.'

"And then she looked at me with her beautiful blue eyes.

" 'You are very young,' she said; 'will you not find the round very fatiguing?'

" 'Oh, no,' I said; 'I love walking.' And then she went indoors."

"How interesting!" exclaimed Twinkles; "you'll make a lot of friends, I expect."

But Muffet laughed.

"If they think about me at all, it will be only that I am a superior village girl. Now let me get on with my story. I went to one or two small, scattered cottages after that, and then I went to a very snug little bungalow near a pine wood. This was on the way home. And here I had another kind of adventure. There was an awful dog loose in the little garden. A kind of mastiff. He barked ferociously, and would not let me open the gate. I'm not easily frightened, but I was in a regular funk. I tried coaxing words and then threats, but he looked as if he would spring at my throat. I was looking round for a stick to defend myself with, when a young man dashed out of a wood shed near the house, and got hold of the dog by the collar. He was without his coat, and his shirtsleeves were rolled up; but I saw at once he was a gentleman. He had been sawing wood.

THERE WAS AN AWFUL DOG LOOSE IN THE GARDEN (Page 47)

"He didn't look at me, but chained the dog up to his kennel.

"'Hurry up!' he said, 'if you have any message.'

"'I am the post,' I said with dignity.

"'The dickens you are!' And then he stared at me and I tried not to laugh, because he looked so very much taken aback. I passed him and was going up to the door, when he said, holding out his hand for the letters, 'For goodness' sake don't knock! She has had a bad night.' So I gave them to him and came away.

"His name is Damers, and he lives with a delicate mother. Kate told me about them. They are quite well off; but she has a weak heart and won't let her son leave her, and he won't be idle, so he teaches mathematics in the grammar school at Mortonbury. That is our nearest town; and it's five miles away. He goes in there on his bicycle four mornings in the week. I should think he was a nice young man to be so good to his mother."

"Go on," said Robin; "any more adventures?"

"I went to a hideous square brick house where I saw nobody but an old man servant, but three old soldiers live there—brothers; one is a General Walpole, another is a Major, and the other only a Captain, but the funny thing is that the Captain is the eldest of them all. He had both his legs broken in the Crimea—or in some wars after it—I forget which. So he retired from the service. They are none of them married, Kate says, but have a sister whom they all bully. She is simply like a housekeeper to them.

"And there is no one young in the neighbourhood," Muffet concluded with a sigh. "So there will be no hockey or tennis for me any more."

"And have you to go round to those houses again this evening?" said Robin. "How sick you will get of it!"

"I shall only go to the big houses. Their newspapers come in the evening. Now, Robin, shall we come into the garden? For I must begin to work in it at once, or we shall have no vegetables at all."

Robin followed her with alacrity, through the little back kitchen out into a narrow strip of forlorn-looking ground, which had been an old potato patch.

"Yes, it looks bad," Muffet admitted, "but John Triggs knew he was going to Canada, so he let his garden go; but I'm going to dig it all myself. Kate wanted me to have a man in and start it, but I told her I was going to be the man. I know lots of girls at school who went in for gardening, and they were taught to dig like common labourers."

"Yes," said Robin wisely, "but you ought to keep yourself fresh for your evening rounds."

"Oh, I shall do all right. I'm as strong as a horse! Look, Robin, I mean to have a flower border each side of the path; we must have flowers. And now come to the orchard."

A little wooden gate led them into a good-sized grassy orchard. The apple trees were already budding, and there were early primroses in the hedge at the bottom. They were not overlooked by any cottages, for their house was the last in the village. Robin drew a long breath of delight.

"I shall spend all the summer out here!" he declared. "All my books shall be written under the apple trees."

Muffet was well pleased with his appreciation.

She took credit to herself for the cottage and its surroundings, and was absurdly happy, and proud of it all. But she declared she had little time to waste, and soon was attacking the potato patch with a big spade and much energy.

Robin went indoors after a little time. He wanted to unpack, and he was longing to be at his writing.

Later in the day Poppet arrived. She was a round-faced, smiling girl, with a very sweet temper, and a very obstinate will. Muffet said it was the only thing she exerted herself about—in having her own way. In all other matters she was placidly indifferent. She was delighted to have left school, and enchanted with the cottage.

That first day was a happy one to them all. But towards the close of it, Robin called Muffet to him.

"Muffet, do you think I'm a prig?"

"No," she said promptly, "you're not."

"Do you remember that dear mother always had morning prayers with us?"

Muffet's face fell.

"Yes—but I think, Robin, it was for the servants, you know; and we've none of them now, and I'm away."

"But religion isn't only meant for servants," said Robin, hesitatingly, "and that small Mary from next door is with us in the morning."

"Then you can read them, Robin," said Muffet in a relieved tone; "it isn't that I don't want to do it; but it isn't quite as much in my line as yours, and I really shall be away. Mother always had them before breakfast."

"I dont *want* to do it," said Robin, truthfully, "because it will remind me so of her; but, Muffet, we mustn't give up the things she cared about."

Muffet gave a short nod.

"All right, we won't, and you shall do it,

Robin. I've got the prayer book she used. It is with your books on the dresser shelf."

"She always seemed," said Robin in his soft, dreamy voice, "to be the link that linked us up to heaven."

"Then you shall be that link now, Robin," said Muffet, moved in spite of her apparent composure. "I can't talk about these things, but I tell you, Robin, that I mean to meet mother again, and I'm going to try to be more like her. I've read my Bible every morning without missing once since she died, and I used to miss scores of times before."

So the next morning the little maid was called in, and Twinkles and Poppet listened, with her, to a Psalm being read, and then very shyly Robin opened his mother's prayer book, and they knelt in prayer together. Neither Twinkles nor Poppet seemed surprised at the proceeding, and family prayer was established in the cottage. None of them knew the effort that it cost their brother, or the many mornings that he would have given worlds to stay in bed for an extra hour's rest, after a sleepless night. But Robin's sense of duty was strong, and if it cost him some pain in his body, it brought peace and comfort to his soul.

CHAPTER IV.

HARD WORK.

For the first few weeks the freshness and novelty of their life kept the girls' spirits up, and Robin's pen was hardly ever out of his hand. The success of his first venture proved most inspiring and inspiriting to him, but gradually difficulties seemed to increase, and life did not present such a rosy hue.

Muffet tired herself over her gardening so much that her post rounds were an effort.

Finally Kate persuaded her to get an old labouring man in for a day's work, and he did more in that one day than Muffet had done in three weeks. Poppet grew lazy, and did not do her share of the house-work satisfactorily. She said she was worked too hard; that Twinkles was like a taskmaster, and was too particular. Money seemed to fly, and Muffet began to have a harrassed look upon her face.

"It isn't what we eat," she said; "we seem to want so many other things. I suppose it is the first start off that is so hard."

"It's our want of management," said Robin, "for we have much more than most of the villagers, and they look happy and cheerful, and well fed! But don't worry, Muffet. I'm at chapter twelve, and when it's finished I'll give you a handsome cheque."

"But we won't run into debt on the strength of it," said Muffet firmly.

Twinkles was the only one of them who kept her gay spirits. She was the life of the cottage. When Kate came in to do some cooking and Twinkles went in to mind her shop, she seemed to get more custom than Kate did the whole day. She had induced Kate to lay in a very good stock of picture post cards, and she had a wonderful way of persuading people to buy them. She was eager to do teas for the holiday people, now Easter was at hand.

Robin at first strongly objected.

"If you could be sure of nice people it would be all right," he said; "but to have a lot of vulgar men and women crowding into our clean kitchen, and ordering you and Muffet about as if you were barmaids, isn't good enough, to my mind!"

Twinkles laughed.

"You shan't see them, Robin. You can stay in your room, or out in the orchard."

And then her brother felt ashamed of himself and offered to help.

The Rector and his wife had called upon them, and their little boy took a violent fancy to Robin. His name was George, but all the village knew him by the title of "Bumbles."

One afternoon he arrived at the cottage by himself. Robin had put up his writing and was alone. When Twinkles and Poppet arrived home from a walk they found an entrancing story being told. Bumbles was sitting on a stool by Robin's side looking quite pale and breathless with excitement.

"Ah!" said Twinkles, "that's how I used to feel in the nursery long ago. Doesn't he know how to make your blood curdle, and your hair stand on end, Bumbles?"

"Oh!" gasped the small boy, "do go on! Tell me more!"

"Not to-day."

Twinkles and Poppet had been into the pine wood, picking up fir cones and sticks for firing. Bumbles looked at their spoil reflectively.

"I s'pose you're pretty poor," he said.

"Very poor," said Twinkles, laughing, "but it doesn't hurt to be poor, Bumbles."

"Mother said she respected Miss Muffet, when Mrs. Blair said she was taking work away from poor people. Mother said you was all poorer than anybody else in the village, for your needs were bigger. What did she mean?"

"That horrid Mrs. Blair!" ejaculated Twinkles. "I can imagine how she talked, but you needn't repeat things to us, Bumbles!"

"I like living here better than at home," the child continued; "you see, we don't laugh as much as you do; there's only mother and me to do it, and father is too good."

"No one is too good to laugh," said Twinkles. "Robin is our good boy, but he laughs like anything. At least he used to, and he will soon again."

"I'd rather be a little naughty," said Bumbles, standing on one leg and staring thoughtfully up at the ceiling. "It's much more fun. Yesterday I harnessed our big dog to the wheelbarrow and got into it and drove him like a horse. We went across the lawn, and left marks, and then across Pitt's new seed beds. That was Carl who did that! But Pitts was awful angry, and I had to be sent to bed after tea. Mother said I must be punished to make me think, but I'm always thinking. I told mother if my think hadn't made me want to do it, I wouldn't have done it. But she didn't seem to understand."

"You shall come out with me in my motor one day," said Robin, looking at him with sparkling eyes. "That will be more fun than riding in a wheelbarrow."

"Oh, let's go to-morrow!"

"No; I must wait till next month. I am busy now."

Robin stifled a sigh as he spoke. He had not

left the cottage, except for a very short walk up and down outside, for nearly a month. And he began to find that life in one room was more cramped than he had expected it to be.

"Are you going to ask me to tea?" questioned Bumbles, changing the conversation suddenly.

"Would your mother like you to stay? Does she know you're here?"

"Oh, I came to the post-office to get some stamps for her. I quite forgot."

"Then off you go at once! She wants those stamps for use before the evening post goes out."

Twinkles bundled him out of the house. Poppet was already laying the table for tea. It was the Thursday before Easter. Bumbles had hardly disappeared, before there was a sharp rap at the door, and when Poppet opened it, there were four girls with their bicycles, demanding tea.

"We used to come here last year," said one of them; "is it a private house now?"

She was looking into the kitchen as she spoke with curious, interested eyes.

"We are still going to do teas," said Twinkles, bustling forward. "Do you want some? How many?"

"Four," said the girl. "What do you charge?"

"Ninepence a head," said Twinkles, promptly; "as much as you want!"

"We used to have it in the orchard," said another girl, "but it would be nicer indoors, if you could manage it."

Twinkles was delighted. She sent Poppet in next door to Kate for two fresh loaves of bread, and further down the street for some clotted cream. There happened to be a fresh baked cake, one of Twinkles' own making. In a very few minutes the girls were sitting down at the table, enjoying plates of bread and butter and jam and cream. They were shop girls from a town some distance off, and perfectly quiet and nice in their manners. From his couch, Robin began to talk to them about the country; and he gleaned some information about good and bad roads for cycling and for motors. They stayed about half an hour, and Twinkles jingled three shillings in her hand delightedly, when they had gone.

"That wasn't much trouble," she said. "I hope some more will come."

"Does it pay?" questioned Robin, sceptically, as he looked at the empty plates on the table.

"Oh, yes; Kate said it did. I will do it all out on paper for Muffet's benefit, and you'll see what profit we make."

Muffet was out on her post rounds. She came in a little tired and cross.

"I wish I wasn't asked to bring back parcels to the post. I'm not obliged to do it, and some of them are so heavy."

"They why do you do it?" said Poppet. "I wouldn't, I know."

"It was Miss Walpole who asked me, and I couldn't say 'no' to her. She had forgotten to post some library books for her brothers. Of course none of them would think of taking them to the post. They make her fetch and carry. She is coming to see you, Robin, one afternoon; she asked me if she might."

"Oh," groaned poor Robin. "I hope I am not going to be a case for visiting. I hate old ladies who come out of pity."

"She isn't like that at all. She is a poor little downtrodden thing, and I would like to give those old men a piece of my mind. Even while she was speaking to me at the door, I heard one of them roaring to her, to let him have the newspaper at once."

Then Muffet was told of the tea, and she was delighted.

"And we'll get a trestle table, and put it out in the orchard, and not have them in our nice kitchen at all," she said.

"But trestle tables cost money," said Robin, doubtfully.

"And it will be such a long way to carry the tea things," said lazy Poppet.

However, Muffet persuaded a village carpenter to knock up a few old planks, and this rough table was duly placed in the orchard. It was well that they did so, for in Easter week they had a good many people passing through the village, and the card in their window always attracted attention. Their tea table was nearly always in requisition, but Muffet said that Twinkles provided too abundant fare. There seemed such small profit for all their trouble.

Still, it kept them busy and happy, and when one day the rector's wife spoke rather depreciatingly to Muffet about it, she replied,

"I assure you, Mrs. Handley, my sisters are quite able to do it and nothing unpleasant has happened. Lots of girls keep tea shops now-a-days, and we find it quite easy."

Mrs. Handley was by way of taking them under her wing. She thought they were all too young to be living together without any older person, and was rather vexed with Muffet's fearless independence.

Robin's second story was finished at last. It was accepted, and he received the sum of twenty pounds for it. On the strength of this twenty pounds, his small motor was overhauled, the necessary petrol bought, and one lovely day, he and Twinkles went for their first ride.

They started after an early lunch, and Robin's delight was great when they got out of the village and began to wind up towards the moor that lay above them.

"I felt I was sinking down into an old man's life," he confided to Twinkles. "This makes me feel as if I'm young again."

"Isn't it delicious? We'll often do it. Now, Robin, let us stop and get out."

They were on the moor now. A grove of great beeches stretched away down a narrow combe. In the distance they caught sight of the sea. Twinkles spread out a light rug they had brought on the short grass.

Already the young bracken was beginning to uncurl, and a blaze of yellow gorse near them scented the air with its sweet fragrance.

"I think, on the whole," said Twinkles, as she lay back on the grass gazing up at the blue sky, "that we are prospering, Robin. I'm getting rather rough hands, 'the horny hands of labour,' you know, and our clothes are becoming shabby, but we never see anyone or go anywhere, so what does it matter? Poppet is so funny! She won't settle down. And she is so careful over her clothes, and not getting her hair untidy, that I sometimes lose patience with her. She always says—'This life can't last all our lives. We shall get out of it soon. Muffet will marry a rich man, or some one will leave us a legacy.' But that's all nonsense, as I tell her. We're poor now, and we shall never be rich."

"Oh, I don't know," said Robin; "what about my books?"

"Well, that will take time, won't it? It's no good for Poppet to be imagining we shall all be rich in a few months' time."

"I wish," said Robin, and his tone was wistful, "that I could come away here by myself. I feel that I might write something bigger; for stillness and beauty always bring big thoughts, don't they?"

"Well, why shouldn't you do it? I do feel sorry for you sometimes in our kitchen, for you hear all the squabbles that go on between Poppet and me, and everybody who comes to the door—there isn't much quiet in the morning. But there is the orchard, you know."

"Yes, I've tried that, and it is all right in the hammock, but you can't call it quiet; the children scream when they come out of school, and peep over the hedge at me, and Kate's cocks and hens annoy me. Oh, I'm a beast to say anything, Twinkles! Compared with you all, I have a very easy time of it; but when I think of a spot like this, it sends wild longings through me. I want to write big things, Twinkles. Things that crowd into my head sometimes, and that I long to put down. I think I could come out here alone, could I not?"

"Of course you could. Your motor is as safe as a church! Come out to-morrow morning, if fine. I'll do up some sandwiches for you, and we won't expect to see you back till tea time."

Then they lay still. Twinkles got drowsy, but Robin's bright eyes were dreamy, and his busy brain worked on. At last he roused his sister, for the afternoon was wearing away, and they were soon merrily spinning down hill towards home. Then suddenly, without any warning, something went wrong with the motor, and after a few ineffectual efforts to make it go, Robin and Twinkles came to a standstill. It was a lonely road. Robin got down, and tried to inspect the works; he lay on his back and tried the different nuts, and screws and gears, but could find no cause for it refusing to go.

Then he sat up and regarded Twinkles ruefully.

"What are we to do?" he said.

Twinkles, as usual, began to laugh.

"Someone must come to our help," she said, "or we must go to someone. We can't stay here all night, nor can you walk home, Robin. I am sure Muffet is at the bottom of this. She cleaned it for you yesterday, and she doesn't know as much as she thinks she does!"

"Well," said Robin philosophically, "let us still enjoy ourselves. Let us sit on the top of this green bank and wait till someone passes by."

They accordingly did so. A pine tree shaded

them over head, and the soft spring air fanned their faces. Robin was tired and heated with his efforts to repair his motor, and sat leaning back against the tree with closed eyes. Twinkles tried to copy his patient example, but it soon proved too much for her.

"I must explore a little, Robin; you sit here still, but I'm positive there must be a cottage or farm within hearing."

She scrambled down the bank and hurried along the road, which was flanked by fields on either side. She had not gone very far before she came to some cross roads, and along one of these she saw, to her great relief, a man in a trap coming towards her.

"I shall make him take Robin home," she said gleefully to herself. But when the trap drew near she was rather dismayed to find that it was a very smart affair, and a gentleman was driving.

She stopped him.

"Do you happen to be passing Coombe Spinney?" she asked.

He pulled up instantly. He was quite young, a handsome smiling youth.

"Yes," he said promptly. "May I have the pleasure of giving you a lift?"

"Oh, it isn't for me, but I have a cripple brother whose motor has broken down, and I don't know how to get him home."

The young man looked a little disappointed, but followed Twinkles, who dashed back to her brother.

And when he saw the plight they were in, he got down from his trap and examined the motor carefully.

"A blacksmith could mend this," he said; "it is only a question of a small screw. I think if I can get a bit out, it would move. And then perhaps you could get on to the smith's at the next village. We are only about two miles from Kistlake."

He set to work, whistling cheerfully. Twinkles held his horse and chattered to Robin.

"Haven't I brought help quickly? Now we shall soon be on our way home. You shall drive in the trap, and I'll take the motor on."

Robin shook his head.

"No, it will be the other way about."

But when the young man had finished his work, he declared that there was plenty of room for three to sit in his trap, and they could tow the motor behind.

This was eventually done. Robin was helped into the trap and then Twinkles got in after him. It was rather a squeeze, but Twinkles made fun of it all, and the young man proved to be very entertaining.

CHAPTER V.

POPPET'S VENTURE.

"It's very *infra dig* for a motor to be towed home by a horse," said Twinkles.

"Horses aren't played out yet, but they're better as beasts of burden than as a means of locomotion. I always bike, but I've been marketing. Made acquaintance with Mortonbury Market? I've been probing fowls and tasting butter, and doing all the things a good housekeeper does! I've a pet old woman there, who wants to set up house with me, on my honour she does! I'm getting rather afraid of her. She tells her cronies 'I'm a praper zort o' veller, with a heart as zoft as her best veather bed!' There's nothing like a recommendation of that sort in a Somersetshire market. Everyone wants me for a customer!"

"I should love to go to market!" said Twinkles, enthusiastically. "If our fowls lay lots of eggs, Robin, what fun it would be to take some in and sell!"

At this moment a carriage and pair passed them. It was the Squire's wife and Lady

Eleanor who were in it. They bowed to the young man. Twinkles was conscious of a curious stare from the younger lady.

Then she turned to their new acquaintance impulsively.

"I wish you would tell me who you are."

"Gascoigne Damers at your service," he responded quickly with a smile.

"Oh, you can't be the good son with the delicate mother?"

"You've hit off my mother, but not me. Now let me guess who you are. You're the good sister of the beautiful post-woman, who lives in the cottage next door to the post-office in the village of Coombe Spinney."

Twinkles laughed gaily.

"Do you call Muffet beautiful? I shall tell her. She is straight and tall, and has a nice colour, but we don't think her very good looking, do we, Robin?"

Robin had been strangely silent. He spoke now with a little effort.

"I think she's just passable," he said.

"I'm thinking," said Gascoigne Damers, "how our acquaintance ought to proceed, because it's going to, you know. My mother is not well enough to call upon you. Will I do instead?"

"Yes," said Twinkles. "You must bring her card, and then Muffet and I will put on our best dresses, and return the visit. And if your mother isn't well enough to see us, we will leave our cards. I suppose we have some, haven't we, Robin ?"

Twinkles' face had sobered now. It seemed such a short time ago that she had seen her mother drive off with her card case in her hand.

"Then I will bring my mother's card to-morrow," Gascoigne said. "I'll make a confession. I nearly came in for some tea the other day. I saw your card up, and you hadn't drawn your blind down. I was at the post-office, and it was raining, and your firelight looked most enticing. Would you have welcomed me ?"

"No, I don't think we should," said Twinkles frankly. "We should have thought you came to pry."

"But you will welcome me to-morrow ?"

"We will," said Twinkles, "for you've proved a friend in need, hasn't he, Robin ?"

"Rather !" said Robin.

Gascoigne drove them up to the post-office, then insisted upon putting the motor by in the little shed close to the house. He and Twinkles parted from each other with mutual liking; and Twinkles began to tell her sisters all that had befallen them.

Later that evening, when Twinkles and Robin chanced to be alone, she said to him,

"Don't you like Mr. Damers, Robin ?"

Robin threw himself back on his cushions with a little impatient sigh.

"Oh, yes, he seems a decent chap—but I can't rave over him—I don't like facetious people!"

"Oh, he isn't facetious, only full of fun."

"I'm a beast," said Robin with conviction. "You know how I feel, Twinkles—always such a stupid poor sort of creature by the side of a fellow like that. It's a kind of mean jealousy—of his strength, and manliness—that I know I shall never have myself. Punch my head, will you? It will make me feel better."

"You're an angel!" exclaimed Twinkles.

"I'd rather be a strong man," said Robin with a whimsical smile.

After a pause, Twinkles said,

"Do you think he really means that Muffet is beautiful, Robin? I wonder if she is."

Robin was about to reply when Muffet came in with some freshly sawn logs for their wood fire. Twinkles looked at her critically, and so did Robin. Muffet had very bright, fearless blue eyes and soft, cloudy golden hair, which she wore in neat coils round a very shapely little head. She had a fresh complexion, and a sweet mouth, and her general appearance was bonny. Robin turned from her to his favourite sister. Twinkles was as tall as Muffet, but much more slender in make; her hair was a dark, curly brown, her eyes a mischievous grey colour with eyelashes which curled up at the ends. She had a white skin but very little colour, and her expression was never the same for two minutes together. But there were depths in Twinkles' nature that were not in Muffet's, and Robin knew it.

"What are you staring at?" said Muffet; "is my face smutty? I have been to the coal cellar."

Twinkles put her arms round her waist and danced round the kitchen with her.

"I know someone who calls you the beautiful post-woman! I'm proud to be your sister, my dear."

"Don't be so nonsensical, Twinkles! And let me go. I must do some accounts."

"Let them go—burn them. They will turn your hair grey if you go on worrying over lost farthings, as you did last night."

"But you don't realise that we're nearly running into debt," said Muffet.

"We're not there yet, Muffet dear; you must get married, or shall we try to marry Poppet to someone? I don't think we could spare you. Poppet wouldn't be missed."

"Poppet is at present sitting on a stool in the back kitchin washing some plates in the sink!" said Muffet, laughing. "Fancy *sitting* by the sink! I told her that her legs were wasted on her. She ought to have been born without any!"

"I wish she'd give them to me," murmured Robin.

"I shouldn't like to have her lying where you do, Robin," said Twinkles with emphasis.

"I can hear all you say," cried Poppet cheerfully from the back kitchen. "A willing horse gets worked to death. I've been on my feet all day and it's poor economy, for it is not only hard on me, but hard on my shoes. And I'm told by Muffet I can't have any new ones till next month!"

There was silence. No one seemed inclined to pursue the conversation.

Twinkles had twinges of conscience. Poppet had such a reputation for laziness that she apparently could never live it down. And Twinkles was so quick herself in action that she was very impatient with Poppet's leisurely ways. As she cast her thoughts back through the day, it did seem as if Poppet had been slowly plodding on at the necessary house work without a break. But nothing seemed to ruffle her composure, and every one believed that she was as placid in heart as in appearance.

The girls had a bed-room each, for, as Muffet said, they were too poor to have any guests to occupy a spare room, unless it was a paying guest, and that did not seem possible at present.

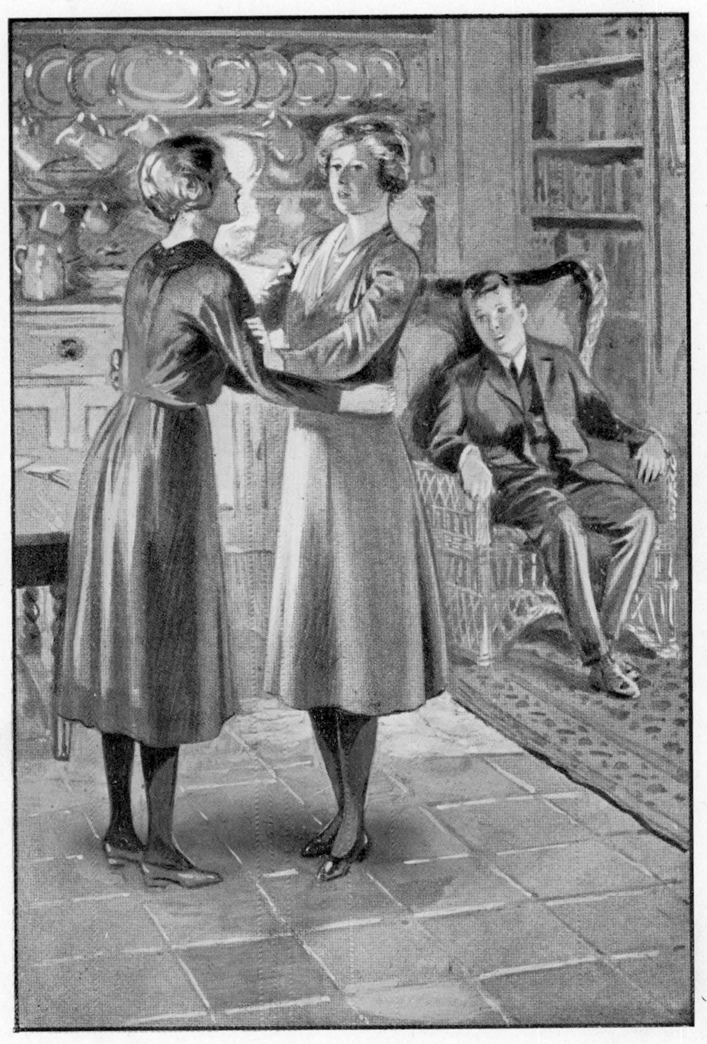

I'M PROUD TO BE YOUR SISTER, MY DEAR. (Page 73)

When Poppet went to bed that night, she cried as if her heart would break.

"Oh, mother, why did you leave us!" she sobbed. "You cared for me. You would have missed me. They want to get rid of me. I slave all day, and yet Twinkles says I wouldn't be missed."

Poppet was very young, and she indulged in much self-commiseration. As she sobbed her heart out under the bed clothes, life seemed black and dismal, and hope and brightness quite impossible. Sleep came to her; and in the morning light things did not look quite so bad. When she knelt down to say her prayers, a sudden determination made her add this petition to them:

"Oh, God, they don't want me here; if anybody wants me in the world, do let me find them out, and go to them." And then she came down stairs with her usual smiling imperturbable face, and set about her morning tasks perhaps a little more silent than usual.

Kate's small maid came in only three times a week now. Poor Muffet was economising as much as possible. Even Robin's extra money did not seem sufficient to make things go easily. And Muffet began to wonder whether Kate's cooking ought not to be discontinued. She did not seem to understand that they ought to be content with labourer's fare, and wanted so many materials for her cooking that Muffet longed to be cook herself. She and Twinkles watched Kate with critical eyes, anxious to learn from her, yet conscious that cakes could be made without cooking butter and with fewer eggs.

This morning was a busy one to Twinkles and Poppet. Kate had come in to help with the washing two days before, and to-day they were ironing and starching. The kitchen was hot. Robin escaped into the orchard. Twinkles scorched her best white blouse and Poppet forgot to clean her iron, and the table cloth got black streaks all over it in consequence.

It was a relief when dinner came, and after the plates and dishes were washed, Muffet said,

"I do wish one of you would help weed the garden. I shall never keep it tidy; the weeds spring up in a night."

"I am going out," announced Poppet.

They stared at her.

"Where?"

"I shan't tell you."

Experience had taught them that Poppet's confidence could not be won when she adopted a high tone.

"I'll help you weed," said Twinkles cheerfully. "Let us work at it for one hour and see who does the most."

Muffet was angry with Poppet.

"I wish you had my job," she said. "I suppose you're going to saunter through the fields picking flowers."

"Perhaps I may," was Poppet's calm response. She left the house soon afterwards, but bent her steps towards the rectory, and when there asked to see Mrs. Handley.

That good lady came bustling into her drawing room, with her hands full of papers.

"Oh, my dear, so glad to see you. I am in the midst of some committee work. Are you all quite well? Nothing wrong, I hope?"

"I wondered if you would help me," said Poppet very steadily. "I want to go away and earn some money."

Mrs. Handley looked at her.

"You are the youngest girl, aren't you? Why, you are not properly grown up. Your hair was down your back yesterday."

Poppet generally plaited her hair in a tail, but to-day she had coiled it round her head.

"I have put my hair up," she said in the same steady, grave voice. "They don't need me at home, Mrs. Handley, and I want to get some work. I am fond of children, and I think I could take care of them. I thought you might know some clergyman's wife who might be glad of me."

"You are very young," said Mrs. Handley, looking at her doubtfully, "but I am always anxious to help those who want to work. The curse of our age at present is the love of ease and pleasure amongst the young. And I do happen to know of a lady who wants a nursery governess for two little girls. But I am afraid she would think you too young."

"She could take me on a month's trial," said Poppet eagerly. Then her face fell.

"I am not clever. I can't teach big children."

"Oh, these are mere babies. Well, I will write to her. She lives at Millsmead Vicarage, five miles from here."

"Could you give me a note of introduction to her, and I would walk over this afternoon? I should be very glad to have it settled before the others know anything about it."

"Have you quarrelled with them?" Mrs. Handley asked, looking at Poppet with keen eyes.

"No, but we seem to get poorer every week, and they can do without me."

"You will never be able to walk there and back."

"Oh, yes, I shall. I will make myself do it. Muffet walks farther than that every day."

Mrs. Handley sat down promptly to her writing table, and scribbled off a note.

As she put it into Poppet's hand she said,

"I don't know anything about you, except

that you are a little lady, and anxious to work. Mrs. Gates is very good at training her servants, so she might be a help to you. Your youth and inexperience is against you, but that she must consider. Good bye, dear, and if you are not successful, let me know."

Poppet marched out of the Rectory with a valiant heart. She felt strung up to do great things, and though the sun was hot, and the roads were dusty, and she was a very bad walker, she accomplished the five miles and arrived at Millsmead Vicarage in due course of time. It was a pretty little old-fashioned Vicarage. The Vicar's wife received her in a pleasant drawing room. She was quite a young woman and something in her tall graceful pose, reminded Poppet of her mother.

Poppet never lost her composure. She neither blushed nor hesitated but went straight to the point.

Her great placidity often made people think her older than she was.

"I should be very glad if you could try me," she said after Mrs. Gates had read the note. "I know I am not as old as I ought to be, but I am very steady and I love children, and I would help you all I can, and not ask a high salary."

Mrs. Gates smiled.

"You are young," she said, "but I like your determination in walking off at once these five miles. You must stay to tea. It is just coming, and we will talk matters over. My little girls are not difficult to manage, but I want a good influence over them. And I want a lady."

Poppet stayed to tea, and before long was telling Mrs. Gates very quietly all about herself. Mrs. Gates said to her husband afterwards, "I know you will think me rash and impulsive, but the girl has such a sweet good face and such grave soft eyes, that I lost my heart to her, and engaged her on the spot. If she disappoints me, she can but go."

Poppet could hardly believe in her good fortune. She trudged back with aching feet, but with a light heart, and she had a girlish pleasure in anticipating the sensation she would cause at home.

"I have arranged it all myself in one afternoon, I will work my very hardest for Mrs. Gates. I love her already. And I shall be much happier earning my living than slaving under Twinkles and being scolded for my laziness. They won't miss me, they said they wouldn't!"

And Poppet really felt very satisfied with her sudden resolve and the successful result of her venture.

CHAPTER VI.

NEW FRIENDS.

When tea time came and went and there was no sign of Poppet, Muffet and Twinkles began to wonder where she was. But the sudden appearance of Gascoigne Damers took their thoughts away from their sister. Gascoigne walked in like a fresh breeze from the moor.

"I've come to call on you," he said, turning to Robin, "and here is my mother's card for your sisters. What a stunning little place you have! Have you overhauled your motor yet? Will you let me do it? I do understand them, but my mother has such a horror of them that we keep the old-fashioned horse to take us about."

He chatted away, and soon Muffet and Twinkles began to feel quite at home with him, and Robin this time showed a little of his quaint humour. They made the old kitchen ring with their laughter. When he got up to go, it was done reluctantly.

"I'll look in again, may I? And will you come and see my mother, Miss Harcourt?"

"Would she really care to see me?" said

Muffet, a little diffidently. "I feel a little shy now I'm the post girl. Of course"—and her head was raised a little proudly—"work of any sort doesn't alter what we are, does it? But your mother may not know about us, and she may think we are pushing ourselves into her house."

"On the contrary," he responded, looking at her steadily, "it would be doing her a favour to visit her. She is ill, and cannot get about. Her heart is very weak, you know, and when I'm away from her the days are long."

"When are you away?" questioned Muffet.

He laughed out.

"Wouldn't you like to know? Can you and your sister come to see her the day after tomorrow?"

"That will be Saturday. Yes, I think we can."

"Of course that's his day at home," said Robin with a chuckle when Gascoigne had left them.

"I hope he will be home," said Twinkles gaily; "for we can't both talk to his mother, and I like him very much.

Muffet said nothing. And it was at this juncture that Poppet appeared.

"Where on earth have you been?" demanded Muffet. "I suppose you have been having tea somewhere."

Poppet nodded, and then sank down exhausted in a chair.

"But I'm very hungry," she added. "Could I have a hunk of bread and cheese?"

Twinkles went away and produced the bread and cheese.

"You've been up to some mischief," she said, standing before Poppet with her arms akimbo, and regarding her critically. "You needn't purse up your mouth as mysteriously, as you will have to confess."

Poppet was already devouring the plateful set before her.

"I have walked ten miles this afternoon," she said. "Have you ever heard of the village of Millsmead? I am going to live there."

Robin and Twinkles laughed uproariously, but Muffet looked anxious.

Poppet enjoyed this mystification.

"Laugh away!" she said. "You say I am no good here, so I am going to leave you."

"I don't think we ever said such a thing," said Muffet; "but a mere schoolgirl like you can't live alone, even if you had the money to do it."

"The mere schoolgirl is going to do what none of you have done yet. She is going to support herself."

"We can't possibly guess," said Robin, "for except for sitting still, and reading story books, we don't know anything that you're particularly good at."

Then his conscience smote him.

"You can work if you will," he added. "Do tell us, Poppet."

Then Poppet launched her bolt.

"I am going the end of next week to Mrs. Gates at Millsmead Vicarage to be nursery governess to her two little girls. I shall live there altogether, and get £20 a year to start with. That will just clothe me."

Twinkles gave a shout.

"*You?* The dunce of your school? A *governess!* Why, Muffet and I wouldn't dare to propose ourselves as that!"

"Nothing venture, nothing have," said Poppet smiling serenely. "I am going, and I shan't be missed!"

"I don't believe a word of it!" said Twinkles. "I don't believe anybody would take you. Why, your hair is down your back! At least, it was yesterday; I see you have put it up now. You have been playing a practical joke on some-one."

"You can believe or not believe what you like," said Poppet, "but it won't make any difference to me. I shall be away from you all this time next week."

Poppet's easy assured tone began to carry conviction with it.

Muffet spoke to her very gently.

"Tell us all about it, dear. We never meant that we didn't want you here. We shall miss you frightfully if you go away, but I don't think you can, unless you get Mr. Maxwell's permission. You are the youngest of us, remember!"

Then Poppet told her story, and her promptness and determination, and the effort to overcome her natural dislike to walking, filled Robin with admiration.

"You shall go!" he said. "I think it is splendid of you! Why, Muffet, she's a little trump!"

There was a good deal of discussion about it all, but when Poppet was in bed that night, Twinkles crept into her room and gave her a hug and a kiss.

"I didn't mean to be nasty! I shall miss you awfully, and it will serve me right! We'll all help you to go, Poppet; but it won't be because we want to lose you, but because it is too good a chance for you to miss!"

Poppet returned the hug and kiss.

"I love Mrs. Gates already," she said in a whisper, "because she reminds me a little of mother. And I mean to get over my laziness and do my very best."

When Twinkles had left her, she lay very still, and her thoughts went back to the prayer she had offered the night before.

It was the first distinct voluntary prayer that Poppet had ever made, beyond the ordinary routine of daily requests, and the speedy answer to it filled her heart with gratitude and love.

"I will be good," she murmered. "I'll help the little girls to be good, too, if I can, and I will try to love and serve God as mother did!"

Mr. Maxwell was written to, but when he heard particulars he wrote his approval, and Muffet and Twinkles had a busy week in helping Poppet with her clothes. There were one or two things she wanted badly, and Muffet considered she ought to have them, even if they made a considerable hole in her purse.

Poppet promised to pay for them out of her own money when she got it.

Mrs. Handley came in and congratulated her.

"She couldn't have a nicer home," she informed Muffet. "Mrs. Gates is a charming woman, and her two little girls are mere babies—no trouble at all. She will treat your sister like a daughter."

So the day came when Poppet departed with her trunk in a farmer's trap, lent for the occasion. Muffet and Twinkles did miss her very much. They had never given her credit for much feeling or enterprise, and this sudden move of hers had astounded and bewildered them. Poppet remained calm and unmoved to the last. Beyond that one confidence to Twinkles, she had refrained from showing her real self to anyone; but she parted from them all affectionately, and promised to write very often.

"And I am within reach of you," she said. "Robin can come and see me in his motor; and if I get a holiday I shall be sure to come over."

Twinkles and Robin were now much together. Muffet was a great deal out of doors, for she spent all her leisure time in the garden, or looking after a brood of chickens which one hen had hatched out in the orchard. These chickens were the joy of her heart.

"They mean eggs and money to me," she would say proudly; and with her own hands she converted an old box into a very nice coop for them.

She was undertaking now to do several commissions for people on her post rounds. And though they had to be done in other times than her post hours, she found she could manage with the help of Robin's motor. She matched wool in the neighbouring town for Miss Walpole. She brought parcels from the station from Lady Eleanor, and once took a basket of eggs to Mortonbury market for a farmer's wife who was ill.

The visit to Mrs. Damer's had been a pleasant one. She was a sweet, frail-looking little woman, perfectly devoted to her big, handsome son; perhaps a little selfish in her monopoly of him, but quite ready to be interested and pleased with the two girls' society.

Robin meanwhile was receiving visitors on his own account. Miss Walpole was perhaps the one who came oftenest. She and he soon formed a quaint friendship, and it began over his writing.

"Ah!" she said, "you're a happy creature to be allowed the full play of your imagination. I often sit and think about it. As a child I made myself either abjectly miserable or riotously happy over it. But I was told that my 'make-ups' were wicked lies; my efforts to write were a waste of precious time; and as I grew older, the desire to produce what was seething in my brain grew less, and at last it died out. So many years of quenching had their fruit. I dare say it is as well. I should have written silly, sentimental stories which would have done no one any good, and yet—yet I don't know!"

She was sitting in the orchard with him as she made these remarks. She was a little plain-featured woman, with grey hair, and rather a big nose, but her eyes, which were an indescribable greeny grey, were alive, and flashed and sparkled with feeling and humour.

"I live in a house of old men," she said, "and I'm an old woman myself, but between you and me and the gate post, I do get some quiet fun out of life. People don't suspect it. They even tell me they pity me. They think I have such a dull life, but you see no one knows about our inner life, do they? And they little know how they amuse me sometimes."

"Go on," pleaded Robin, "I love to hear you talk. I do like anyone who sees the funny side of things."

"But I want to talk to you seriously. You are young, and life is before you, and I expect you have high ideals."

"I don't know about life," said Robin, stifling a little sigh. "Life as you mean it will never befall me. I shall be tied like a woman to a couch, and to indoor pursuits!"

"But your soul is not tied," said Miss Walpole.

"No," responded Robin, with one of his brilliant smiles, "and that part of me does get away."

Miss Walpole put her hand on his arm impressively.

"Live up to your ideals, my boy, and let your writing be the outcome of it. Don't send out stuff that will perish. Let it be immortal, living on in the hearts and lives of men and women, long after you have passed away!"

The fire was in her eyes, and a flush upon her cheeks as she spoke. Robin's heart glowed within him. Then he sighed.

"I write for money, Miss Walpole—more stories of adventure and daring for boys."

"I don't care what you write. You can raise boys' thoughts to what is good and noble. See that you don't miss your opportunity."

"I'm only a scribbler," Robin murmured again.

"Aim higher!"

And then Miss Walpole gave a little laugh.

"If I could put myself back to your age, I should be writing twaddle, but I had no one to tell me how to write, no one to show me what a power a ready pen could be. You have been set apart from your kind for a purpose. Perhaps the purpose is that you should sway men's hearts by your pen."

"Oh, if I could think so! But I have been set apart to suffer, Miss Walpole. I should like to tell you a little allegory of my mother's which has comforted me ever since I was a tiny chap, and fled to her arms when in pain."

Robin recited in hushed tones the story which, as a little boy, his mother had told to him.

"The golden gates of the city on the hill were open; the glorious sunshine seemed dazzling to those who were without; the brightness of those gates was almost overpowering. Under the shade of some beautiful trees was a radiant throng. They were all gathered there in the sunshine on the top of that wonderful golden hill. Such a long, long line of white-robed little children, ready to go down into the big, busy world below. The King was there himself, and by Him was an open book, and one of the King's trusted servants was writing in it. Then one by one the children were called before their King, and the page in the book was opened which bore their name upon it. They were sorted into little bands, and each band was given a banner, and before they marched down the hill, the King put up His Hands and blessed them. The first band which started was the knights, and the King said to them:

" 'I send you forth to fight against the evil powers, to be champions of the weak and oppressed. The fight will be long and hard; for cruelty, injustice, oppression, and tyranny will last as long as the world lasts. Your heritage is warfare; a crusade against all that is wrong; the world has need of you. Go, and your banner reminds you that I am with you.'

"Their crimson banner bore the words: 'Be strong, and of a good courage. I will be with thee.'

"The next band was the labourers.

"'Your heritage is labour,' said the King. 'I send you forth to labour; your life will be spent in it, and labour of mind and body is an honourable calling. Work with content, remembering that it is your heritage, and that your work will not be in vain.'

"Their banner was a blue one: 'Be strong and work, for I am with you.'

"The knights had marched away with strong purpose on their young faces: the labourers marched after them with the same sturdy joy, and now came a band of children with wonderful shining eyes.

"'Your heritage is genius,' said the King. 'Go down into the world to quicken the intellects, to cheer the sad, to find cures for the many evils that surround you, and to ennoble the aims and ambitions of the dull and slothful.'

"Their banner was a silver one: 'The wise and their work are in the hand of God.'

"They marched away and the company of children became smaller.

"The next band was called to the heritage of teaching; and on their tiny faces was already the stamp of holy gravity.

"The King reminded them of their high calling, their possibilities of influence, their power for good and for evil.

"'You go forth as My teachers, to teach of Me and to draw men into My Kingdom.'

"Their banner was a snowwhite one with the words: 'I will be with thy mouth and teach thee what thou shalt say.'

"Then came the band which was called to the heritage of rulers. There was already the stamp of dignity and strength upon their soft baby faces.

"'Go forth and rule,' said the King; 'and let your rule be an ever-just and righteous one, suppressing evil, and maintaining My Laws. Live for those you rule, and let their rights be considered as your own.'

"Their banner was a purple one, and bore these words: 'He that ruleth over men must be just, ruling in the fear of God.'

"Another band there was who marched away from their King.

"'Go down into the world,' He said unto them; 'there are many who will need your pitying, loving care: little ones who know no parents' love; old people nearing the valley of the shadow of death; the sick, the poor, the weak and the erring—all are waiting for those who will take care of them. It may not be great work; it may not bring you fame; but it will bring you these words of commendation when your work is done: 'Inasmuch as ye have done it unto one of the least of these My brethren, ye have done it unto Me.'

"And these words were upon their green

banner as they marched away; and their eyes were full of love and pity for all the world who wanted tender care.

"Then the last little band came up; and over the King's face came a wondrously soft and tender smile.

"'My little ones,' He said, 'My chosen ones, I have called you to the highest heritage of all; it is to the heritage of suffering. No other heritage will bring so much gain and glory as this, and it was the heritage that your King's Son chose Himself, and took upon Him when He went down to tread the busy world below. Go forth and suffer, and with every pang you feel, remember that it is the highest service for your King.'

"Their banner was a golden one, and the shining glory of it almost hid the words upon it: 'Rejoicing that they were counted worthy to suffer.'

"Before they marched away, the King did what He had not done to the others: He called up each child separately, and laid His Hands upon his head and blessed him.

"And this little band trod the downhill path with some of the glory of their King reflected in their faces, and not one of the weakest and smallest of them there would have changed their heritage for all the world; for had not the King given them the heritage of His Only Best Beloved Son."

There was silence when Robin paused. He could never repeat his mother's beautiful story without being affected by it. The words were burnt into his very soul.

Miss Walpole wiped her wet eyes.

"It's beautiful. Write it out for me. I'm in that band at present, and the care of three old bachelor brothers ought to be a beautiful charge!"

She went away smiling, and Robin lay still and thought. When Twinkles came to him half an hour afterwards, she found he had done no writing.

"I've just been learning this afternoon," he said to her. "It won't be waste of time. Oh, Twinkles, do you think that I could ever leave these boys' stories and write in a great way? Sometimes I almost feel I could write poems!"

"I expect you could; you've written rhymes, haven't you? But poetry doesn't pay like stories."

"Oh," said Robin, rolling himself out of his hammock and taking up his crutches, "money isn't everything, Twinkles!"

"No, but it is a good deal to us at present. Don't try to run before you can walk, Robin. You'll write big things when you get older, I know you will, but you have plenty of time."

"I don't know," said Robin, raising his face thoughtfully to the pale evening sky. "I may not have a long life before me!"

Twinkles put her arm round him affectionately.

"Robin, do you remember mother scolding you for wishing to have a short life? She said we mustn't wish to shorten our opportunities for work. You make me miserable when you talk so. Now I'll tell you something to make you laugh."

She began to give him a funny account of some old women who wanted to send money up to London to their daughters, and came to the post office to have it explained to them. Twinkles was in charge, and she had rather an amusing time with them. Robin's laugh rang out merrily, and for the time he was his happy self again.

It was always Twinkles' way to make people laugh. If she ever said a grave word, it was quickly followed by a jest. Now that Poppet had gone, Twinkles found her work heavier in the house, but she made light of her difficulties, and laughed when she was most tired.

Muffet got impatient with her sometimes.

"Don't you realize that we're too poor to be so frivolous?" she would say.

"A tramp on the way to the workhouse may have his joke," returned Twinkles, "and so shall I!"

CHAPTER VII.

THE FIDDLER.

"Let me carry your bag."

"No, thank you."

"I insist."

"You won't have it. It is against orders."

"Bosh!"

"I am responsible for the post bag, and am never supposed to let anyone else touch it."

"Do you think I would steal the contents?"

"You might drop or lose them."

"Am I safe to walk by your side?"

This conversation took place between five and six one afternoon in the beginning of July. It had been a very hot day, and Muffet was feeling the weight of her post bag. She wore a shady hat, but her fair face was flushed underneath it, and Gascoigne in his white flannels looked cool enough and strong enough to carry her and her burden together. They were walking along the dusty high road. Gascoigne tilted back his straw hat and began to grumble.

"Girls are so ridiculous now-a-days. Their education and training has been sheer folly. Women don't need to be independent of men.

That's the reason they don't marry. Men won't have masterful wives. No man in his senses would. He wants a woman to be a woman, not an effeminate man."

"Go on," said Muffet, in a superior tone; "I like to hear you."

"If I had a wife," said Gascoigne, swishing off the grass heads by the roadside as he passed by, "I should make her clearly understand that in civilised countries man was born to bear and carry burdens, women were born——"

"To sit and smile," broke in Muffet. "A doll would suit you, a sawdust figure, or one of those automatic figures which wind up to order!"

"Don't be huffy, Miss Harcourt. Let us talk about my future wife. I mean to have one, some day."

"She does not interest me," said Muffet, loftily.

"I don't want a puppet," Gascoigne went on gravely, "but I do want a womanly woman who will be proud of her sex and keep to it."

"And who will have no will or individuality of her own, but be a weak echo of her lord and master," said Muffet scornfully. "There are two types of men in the world whom I heartily dislike. One is a tyrant and bully who thinks that his will is law, and woman his vassal and slave, the other a fop and dandy who can't do a day's work to save his life and thinks every girl he comes across must be in love with him."

"You're a scornful young woman!"

Gascoigne's temper was unruffled, but then he was not carrying a heavy post bag.

There was silence for a few moments, then he adopted a different tone.

"Do be nice to me, Miss Harcourt. It is too warm a day to quarrel. When I joined you I was full of pity for you!"

"And I hate your pity!"

Muffet's tone was still wrathful.

"Then I'm sorry I mentioned it. I was also full of admiration for you. And as my way was the same as yours, I hoped we might enjoy our way together."

"Well, let us do it, then," said Muffet, smiling up at him frankly. "I'm not really cross, but I won't be helped."

Gascoigne wisely let this challenge drop, and they began to chat together in a more friendly spirit. When Muffet came to the Hall, she said:

"I know you're going to play tennis here. I would so much rather you went on in front of me. Don't let us walk up the drive together. Mrs. Blair is not very nice to us, and it will only make her talk."

Gascoigne at first objected, but seeing that Muffet would really feel uncomfortable if he persisted in accompanying her, he raised his cap and strode on. She gave a sigh of relief. Gascoigne was by this time a great friend. He would drop in at the cottage all times of the day, and Robin's first dislike to him had changed into hearty liking.

Muffet and Twinkles both liked him; he seemed to be able to put his hand to anything. He would help Muffet in the garden and Twinkles in the house. Whether it was carpentering, or digging, or washing up tea things, he was an adept at it all. And he was as great a hand at talking as at doing.

Muffet watched him stride across the lawn to a group of gaily clad people who were lounging in chairs near the tennis court, and a quick sigh escaped her.

"It wasn't so very long ago that I was enjoying tennis parties, and now I am supposed to be quite an inferior being, not fit to associate with gentle people. How hateful it is to be poor! And of course I have made it worse by being a post-girl. Well, I won't be discontented."

She marched on to the house and delivered her letters, then took the short cut through the grounds which led to Lady Eleanor Blair's. She found the old lady in her garden, and she beckoned to the girl to come across the lawn to where she was sitting under an acacia tree.

"Good evening. You can leave my letters here; it will save you a few steps. You look tired."

Muffet did not often get much sympathy, but Lady Eleanor had always been pleasant to her.

"I am rather warm," Muffet said.

She handed the letters to Lady Eleanor as she spoke, and was surprised to see her start and tremble as she took a foreign letter from her and opened it.

Muffet was just shutting up her bag and turning to go when she was addressed by Lady Blair.

"Wait a moment. I may have to send a telegram. Could you take it back with you?"

"We don't send telegrams from our post-office, but I will certainly take it back and give it to Bob Cross. He is the lad whom Kate always trusts with them, and he would take it right on to Mortonbury."

Lady Eleanor's hand was trembling as she wrote on a sheet of paper near her.

She asked Muffet to count the words.

They were addressed to a London Hotel, and ran as follows:—

Come home. I have wanted you.

C. Blair.

And then she said very gently,

"I should like it to go to-night; it is to one of my sons who has been abroad for many years."

"I will take it at once," Muffet said cheerfully.

She finished her rounds, wondering that she had not heard about Lady Eleanor's youngest son, and then she despatched the telegram and opened the door of her cottage with a sigh of relief. The scene that met her eyes astonished her.

Robin lay on his couch with his eyes ablaze, and a happy smile about his face. In the recess between fire and window opposite him, stood a young man playing a mad, weird strain upon a violin.

He was resting his head against the wall as he played. The square table was pushed back against the wall, and in the middle of the kitchen up and down and round and round, was Twinkles dancing with Bumbles. The music and the dancers seemed to be having a race with time; but when Muffet closed the door behind her with a bang, they all came to a standstill. A crashing discord on the violin, and then the young man was bowing to Muffet, and Twinkles had thrown herself into a chair quite exhausted. Bumbles caught up his cap, which was lying on the table.

"I'm going, Miss Muffet. We've been having such fun! I only stayed for one dance more. I think it's the Pied Piper. Our feet wouldn't keep still!"

He darted out of the door, for he had overstayed his time. Robin introduced the stranger.

"Mr. Allister wanted some tea, and as he had his violin with him, he has been playing to us."

"I think you've all gone mad," said Muffet, briefly.

Then she smiled one of her sweet smiles upon the stranger.

"My brother is very fond of music; he hears none now we have no piano."

"And none of us is really musical," put in Twinkles, breathlessly. "At least, I adore listening to it, but I'm a bad hand at playing, am I not, Robin? Now, Muffet, sit down, and Mr. Allister will play you something that will rest and soothe you. Do play again that thing that made us cry."

Mr. Allister smiled, and tucked his violin under his chin again. Muffet looked at him critically.

He was dressed in a loose blue serge suit, with a white flannel shirt and a flaming orange silk tie, which was tied in a big bow, and looked foreign in texture. He had a small, delicately cut face, with beautiful dark eyes, and a dark, well-cropped head of hair. His hands and long taper fingers were distinctly those of a musician. If he had had long hair, he would have fulfilled the type of a vagabond musician, and yet as it was, there was something in his pose and manner that gave the impression of good birth and breeding.

He began to play; Muffet caught her breath and listened. As Twinkles had said, none of them had musical abilities, but as little children they had always been entranced by their mother's music.

And now such sweet pathetic sounds came stealing out of the violin that Muffet gave herself up to the pleasure of listening to it. Then from the corner came a rather gruff voice:

"It is a maid wandering in the forest searching for her lover. He has been slain by a wild boar. She finds his body, which the boar has abandoned."

As Muffet listened, she felt a strange lump come in her throat. Robin and Twinkles were following every note. Robin saw the great forest, he heard the quivering of the breeze through the trees, the crackle of the twigs underfoot, as the girl sped on her sad quest. The longing of an aching soul, the passion of a desperate love, and the despair of a broken heart was all there. It took Robin right away from the kitchen into another world. He saw the girl in a crumpled heap upon the ground, with her arms round the lifeless body of her lover, and her tears raining upon his poor dead face. And then came a solemn requiem for the departed spirit.

When the last notes died away, Robin lay back with enraptured face. Muffet winked some wet drops from her eyelashes. And the young man laid his violin on the table.

"I have asked," he said, breaking in upon the silence, "if you can give me a bed-room for the night. I was told I must wait till you came home."

He addressed Muffet.

"We don't take in lodgers," she said hastily; "but there is a room at the post-office next door that you can have."

"Don't be stiff, Muffet," said Twinkles. "We are all the greatest friends. He has just come from Italy, and is passing through our village to regale himself once again with English country. I've begged him to make a long stay here and come in and play to Robin every day. And he thinks our room a perfect specimen of a cottage home."

"You will be kind to a wanderer," Mr. Allister said, looking at Muffet with pathetic eyes. "Your sister and brother have charmed me. They have taken me to their hearts, and given me a most friendly welcome. And those who love my violin better than me are the ones I want to be with!"

"But what am I to say?" said Muffet, looking at Twinkles perplexedly. "Your music is delightful, but you are a stranger to us."

"I am respectable and I have paid for my tea. But let me have breakfast with you to-morrow. Let us have it in the orchard. Who would be under a roof when the morning dew is on the grass, and the music of the birds steals away one's heart?"

Twinkles laughed.

"We will have it in the orchard. It will be a delicious change. Are you going?"

"Yes, your sister is suspicious of me. But she will be friends with me soon. She is too young to be obdurate."

Then with another little bow he left them, and they heard him talking to Kate, next door.

Twinkles laughed again.

"He is a perfect dear; why don't you like him, Muffet! He might be a minstrel on a stage, or a troubadour. He is unlike anyone I have ever seen. And his music is heavenly. It was so funny! Robin and I were having a growl together just before he arrived; we were dull. Robin could not get ideas for his stories, I was sick of the constant dish washing. The kitchen seemed hot and stuffy, the flies were buzzing, and then suddenly—a knock at the door—and in he walked. And in a few minutes Robin and I were in Italy with him, hearing the mandolines and guitars going under the palms by the blue sea, and seeing the oleanders and the roses and the marble palaces. Then he asked for tea, and after it was over he played. Bumbles came in with a message from his mother, who said he must not stay, but the violin began to play frolicking dances, and Bumbles and I ran into each others' arms, and then we were dancing for our lives. It almost seems unreal now he is gone. He bewitches with his music!"

"He inspires!" cried Robin. "You must let him be friends with us, Muffet. You must be kind to him. I don't care who he is, and what he is, I only know he has put fresh life into me, and made the world a happy place to me."

"Kate will look after him," said Muffet in her practical way; "he will be moving on to-morrow, I expect. If he likes to come to breakfast we can give it to him, but I'm not going to have it in the orchard. Why should we attend to the vagaries of a superior tramp?"

"Oh, you're so deadly matter of fact," said Robin, half amused, half vexed. "Twinkles and I get carried off our feet by any originality. We have got into such a straight, narrow rut, that if we swerve aside from it, you think it awful. Don't be a grandmother, old Muffet, don't get wrinkles before your time. If he is a tramp, he is a gentlemanly one, and if I had legs like you I would be off with him to-morrow."

Muffet laughed merrily. Kate often said she was getting old before her time. Household cares weighed on her spirit, but she looked young enough now.

"We don't want you to run away from us, Cock Robin! But get inspired as much as you like. Oh, dear! I am so very, very tired. I used to pity postmen in the winter when the weather was rough and wet, but now I know that summer is the most trying time."

"I'll get you a glass of lemonade," said Twinkles. "Don't look shocked. I've made some to-day. It's a fresh venture, and I've sold six glasses to different cyclists passing by. Didn't you see my card in the window, 'Fresh Lemonade'? And there are just two glasses left. I don't feel a bit tired now! I wish I could have danced a little longer!"

She went off in quest of the lemonade, singing under her breath, and Muffet said with a sigh,

"I wonder if it is worth it?"

"What?" enquired Robin.

"Oh, this post business! I'm so dead sick of it. It's so monotonous."

"Don't be growsy! Why, I think it must be so jolly interesting. Think of what you take in your hands. You may be bringing a fortune to someone! Life and death go through the post"—here Robin's eyes grew dreamy. "A letter may alter a person's life in one moment. It may bring disaster, it may bring joy. I should like to write the autobiography of a letter bag."

Muffet's eyes grew brighter.

"Sometimes it's interesting. This afternoon Lady Eleanor had some good news. I'm so glad; for she is so sweet. I feel I could love her. I won't be discontented, but I just long sometimes to be like other girls. I saw them all playing tennis at the Hall. Gascoigne Damers went there."

"It's hard luck on you!" said Robin; "but you just wait a bit. I'll write on, and get money and we'll enjoy ourselves. I feel I can do anything since I've heard that music!"

Mr. Allister had certainly brought good to Robin. If Muffet felt her heart sink sometimes Robin certainly did too. He had his fits of depression to combat with, as well as his physical aches and pains. But to-night he was jubilant, and Twinkles and he refused to let Muffet sit still and groan. Before they retired to bed, she was rested and comforted, and was her brave smiling self again.

CHAPTER VIII.

LITERARY DIFFICULTIES.

Kate informed them the next morning that after engaging a bed room, and having a bit of supper the violin player had gone out in the dusk and had never come back.

"He is just one of these travelling gentlemen who never know their own mind, and tour round for pleasure. I always have my doubts when I see a knapsack, because it means moving on when the spirit seizes them. 'Tis a good thing I didn't get any fish or sausages in for his breakfast. As it is, he paid for his supper and bed in advance, and he'll be the loser, not me!"

"But," said Twinkles, "you oughtn't to take his money for a bed-room if he didn't use it."

"Well, what will I please to do?" enquired Kate.

"Perhaps he may come back again. I hope he will. I was longing for him to play again, and he was going to breakfast with us, Kate, and I was going to make an omelette. It is a pity; Robin will be disappointed."

But that evening when Muffet went her round

with her letters, she had a great surprise. When she got to Lady Eleanor's she saw her standing outside the hall door on the broad stone steps talking most eagerly to a tall, thin man, and that man was Mr. Allister. They both turned as Muffet came up the steps. Lady Eleanor smiled at Muffet.

"My telegram was too late," she said. "My boy was already on the way home."

"I am so glad," Muffet murmured, hardly knowing what to say.

Mr. Allister held out his hand.

"Good morning, Miss Harcourt. I hope you did not wait breakfast for me. I have told my mother that I have friends already in the village, and I am going to bring her to see your family genius. Shall we say this afternoon?"

"My dear Allister," murmured his mother, "you must see your brother—and Clare."

"All right. I'm back in the conventional world, so will place myself in your hands."

Muffet left her letters, without any more conversation. Her news when she returned home astounded Robin and Twinkles.

"How on earth could he stay away from his mother when he was so close to her?"

"And why did he pretend to be what he wasn't?" demanded Twinkles.

They could not unravel the mystery, but the

next afternoon Mr. Allister appeared with Lady Eleanor and in a confidential aside to Twinkles told her all she wished to know.

"I had been a bad boy—stayed away for fifteen years—couldn't hit it off with my brother, and my mother wanted me to go into the Church. It was altogether too much for me. Had some words with good respectable George, and he turned me out of the house. He was going to marry, and found it a good opportunity to do it. So off I went with my fiddle, and have had some grand times since. Played in the orchestra at Vienna at various operas, and then drifted into Italy. I only heard lately my mother was living alone, so I thought I would like to see her, and as I wasn't sure how the land lay, I determined to put up in the village before I presented myself. I did honestly mean to sleep at the post-office, but I took a moonlight stroll and saw my mother walking on her terrace, so of course I joined her. Now, have I explained myself?"

"Quite," said Twinkles promptly. "I hope you'll play to us again."

Lady Eleanor was already losing her heart to Robin. She told her son afterwards he had the face of an angel. The daintiness of the little kitchen, the freshness and simplicity of Twinkles, and perhaps the sight of a beautiful miniature of their mother hanging up on the wall, was a revelation to her and delighted her heart.

When Muffet was summoned in from the garden and she saw her beautiful Lady Eleanor chatting to Robin, she crimsoned with pleasure.

Robin had told Lady Eleanor all about themselves, and she told him she had once known his father.

She held out her hand to Muffet, with her sweet gracious smile.

"You are brave young people," she said; "I am sorry I have not discovered you before, but I live so quietly and come so seldom into the village that I did not realise your whereabouts."

She did not stay very long, but her son lingered behind her, and went out into the orchard with Robin, and smoked a pipe and talked of many things. Then he insisted upon helping Muffet to garden.

"I love the simple life," he said, "not as a fad and recreation as the London folk do, but as a rule of life. People think a musician's hand useless for all else—but mine have tilled and delved with the Italian peasants, and even helped to build with stones and mortar when I was hard pushed. Why should we, because we live on a little conventional island, settle in our own feeble brains what is becoming and right for one class to do, and bring up an effeminate self-indulgent race of beings? If a lord likes to keep a shop, and his footman likes to ride in the Row why shouldn't they do it? Why shouldn't any Englishman be free to do what is pleasing to him?"

"Are you a Socialist?" asked Muffet, regarding him gravely.

"What is a Socialist? I don't know. Nobody knows. One man means one thing, one another. I hate slavery being tied down to rules of custom and society. I like a free land."

"Where everybody goes their own way without any consideration for anybody else," said Muffet. "But that wouldn't be good citizenship. Everybody ought to be able to bear restraint, and endure discipline. Otherwise they do become an effeminate, self-indulgent race!"

Allister looked at her thoughtfully.

"My creed is happiness," he said.

"But you haven't found it in doing only what you like, without reference to anyone else?"

"You are a little moralist. I'm what they call a 'bad lot,' therefore a happy lot. I am happy. I defy anyone to make me otherwise." He laughed so merrily that Muffet smiled at him sympathetically.

"I don't expect you are really selfish," she said, "or bad. You only like to pretend you are."

Muffet was very near the truth, but Allister shook his head.

"I'm bad, and mad, and everything I ought not to be until I get my fiddle into my hands. He is my good angel. I am permeated with goodness and virtue when he begins to speak. He led me back to my mother."

"He was a long time doing it," said Muffet, severely.

"I suppose he was, but I was a cub when I left home, and wanted licking into shape. He kept me away till that was in progress."

Allister was speaking gravely now. He and Muffet were thinning out a carrot bed.

"Do you think I am shapely yet?" he asked her whimsically.

"No," said Muffet, promptly; "you must learn to like restraint—or at all events to endure it, and you must not act on impulse. It is a sign of an ill-regulated mind. There! That is my sermon, word for word what they used to say to us at school."

"Do go on; tell me more. I'll make my fiddle tell you the story of an ill-regulated soul being licked into shape."

"I have no more to say except to ask you to bring your violin soon and play to Robin."

"And to you," he said. "You are apparently a hard, practical piece of virtue, but my fiddle squeezes tears out of stone, and you are not inaccessible."

"I should hope not. Oh, Mr. Allister, am I hard? Everybody seems to think I am! But it's only that things have to be done, and I'm the strongest to do them."

There was a wistful look in Muffet's eyes not often seen by her brother or sisters.

Allister held out his hand.

"Good-bye. I'm going—at least, after I've washed my hands. What a pity we can't have sand instead of earth. It's so much cleaner."

In the days that followed, Allister was very often at the cottage. Gascoigne Damers and he often met each other there, but there was not much cordiality between them.

Twinkles and Robin used to discuss them laughingly together.

"I'm sure they both like Muffet," Twinkles said one evening, when Muffet had retired unusually early to bed, and she and Robin were sitting together over a smouldering fire in the kitchen.

"Why should they?" Robin said wonderingly.

"Oh, she is so fresh, so beautiful, and has such a grace and air about her. Muffet is more like dear mother than any of us. Men like beauty. They won't have the patience to look for anything else."

Twinkles spoke with the assured wisdom of youth.

"I prefer the look of you," said Robin.

Twinkles laughed.

"That's nice of you. But they don't. Never mind. You and I will grow old together. I shall always keep house for you, Robin."

"If I have a house to keep," said Robin, rather despondently. "It takes a lot to live, Twinkles, doesn't it? And since I heard that my publisher doesn't want another book from me yet awhile, I am wondering how we shall get on."

"Oh, splendidly!" said Twinkles, her eyes beginning to gleam, for she rarely failed to hearten Robin up when he was low-spirited.

"To begin with, you must go on writing and find another publisher. That's easily done. When you can put 'Author of' after your name, it makes a lot of difference. Then Muffet will marry. Who will she have, do you think? Gascoigne will be the best off, for he will come into an uncle's property one day; but Allister is the most amusing because you never know what he's going to say. Then, when you and I are left together, we shan't have so many expenses, and we shall be getting rent from home in about another year. We shan't starve, Robin. And I've any amount of plans in my head for making money, when the summer is over."

Certainly it might have misled others besides Twinkles to watch the two young men come in and out so constantly. Muffet was grave and unimpressionable. She scolded Allister for his lazy and inconsequent views of life, she argued with Gascoigne on the question of male or female supremacy. But when Lady Eleanor asked her to come to a garden party she refused, and she did the same when Mrs. Damer asked her to dinner. Twinkles told everybody she never left Robin. Muffet considered it bad taste to ask them out at all, so soon after their mother's death. And soon, people saw that the young people were best left alone.

"I think we have a good many friends," Robin announced one day at tea. "I've had Miss Walpole here for more than an hour this afternoon; she's an awfully decent sort. But I'm certain those old chaps lead her a dog's life."

"I like Lady Eleanor best," said Muffet. "She always talks to me now when she sees me coming with the letters in the evening. I feel I could kneel down and worship her, when she puts her hand on my shoulders and looks at me with her kind, sweet eyes."

"She frightens me," said Twinkles. "I like Mrs. Damers best. I don't wonder Gascoigne is so devoted to her. I took her some of our plums to-day—you said I might, Muffet—and she made me sit by her, and talk nonsense. She said it did her good."

"It's funny—two mothers living close to us with their sons," said Muffet.

"Gascoigne is the best son," said Twinkles; "Allister will be off soon; he is too restless to stay here, and he doesn't hit it off with his brother, I know."

"That isn't his fault," said Muffet warningly; "he is the essence of good temper."

"Oh, you always take his part behind his back."

One afternoon, Poppet surprised them by walking in. Mrs. Gates had driven over to call at the Hall and had brought Poppet with her as far as the village. Poppet was in very good spirits.

Twinkles eyed her curiously.

"What do you do with your pupils? Do you do anything but eat and sleep? You haven't grown any thinner, Poppet!"

Poppet smiled serenely.

"I do a lot of things. I have been helping Mrs. Gates to make jam this morning, besides the children's lessons. I am enjoying it all, and Mrs. Gates treats me like an eldest daughter. You ask her if I do nothing but sleep and eat! You all gave me that character years ago, and if I worked myself to the bone at home, you would still say it. But I don't mind a bit, now that I am away from it. You are not looking well, Twinkles!"

"I'm perfectly fit," said Twinkles, "only the oven and I have been at war to-day. It determined to spoil everything I put in it. Kate is laid up with an attack of rheumatism, and I've been in and out minding her shop besides doing our cooking. Muffet had to go to town to do some shopping, so she couldn't help."

Then Poppet produced very proudly a half sovereign, which she laid on the table.

"My contribution towards housekeeping," she said. "I was paid my salary yesterday. I've had to keep the rest to get some clothes I want."

"Muffet will be delighted," sighed Twinkles. "It must be very nice to earn money. I'm the only one who doesn't do it. I'm a caretaker, like Miss Walpole, am I not, Robin? I suppose that is to be my rôle through life. Now tell us more about your situation, Poppet."

"It sounds as if I were a servant!" remarked Poppet, but she complied with Twinkles' request, and seemed to have a good deal to say for herself. She had gained in assurance of manner and seemed to have lost all her schoolgirl ways. Muffet came in before she left, and the three sisters were very happy together. When Poppet departed, Muffet and Twinkles agreed that she had improved in every way, and were quite satisfied in the wisdom of her choice.

Robin shook his head gravely.

"If I were a genius, I should work for my sisters, not they for me."

Poor Robin was not finding the literary path very smooth to his feet. He was writing too constantly, too fast to turn out good work. He wrote with aching head and back, working himself into a nervous fever till he had finished his tale. And his last story had been returned to him by a hard-hearted publisher, with this terse ultimatum, "Declined with thanks."

He was now trying some short poems. The spell of Allister's violin had produced them. But his health was not so good, and he was having sleepless nights. Twinkles watched him with an anxious eye and heavy heart. She knew that the urgent need of money was driving him beyond his powers. And if Muffet was harassed and anxious over her accounts, and over the difficulty of making both ends meet, Twinkles was terribly uneasy over her favourite brother.

Mr. Maxwell had been very kind and had advanced them money when Muffet had informed him they could not keep within their income. She kept saying to herself, that this first year would be the worst, that the next they would be receiving rent for their house, but as the summer drew to a close and she thought of the extra costs of lights necessary during the winter, her heart sank within her. All this Robin knew, and he was bitterly disappointed that he could earn so little. Twinkles read his poems with much appreciation.

"They will live, Robin. Poetry lives much longer than boy's adventurous tales. I wish you would let Allister hear them. He would be such a good judge."

But Robin could not be persuaded at present to let any outsider see his first attempts at poetry.

CHAPTER IX.

IN THE ORCHARD.

Twinkles was very busy in the orchard picking apples. It was a lovely afternoon in September. She had a pink cotton sunbonnet on her head, and little dark curls were flying out over her sparkling face. She was thoroughly enjoying herself. Robin had gone out in his motor and Muffet was with him. It was unusual for her to be his companion, but she was looking tired and fagged, and Twinkles knew that her evening round would be an effort after a hard afternoon at apple picking. As Twinkles worked she sang little snatches of songs to herself. Suddenly a voice the other side of the fence made her pause.

"May I help you? Or shall I spoil the picture?"

It was Allister Blair. His violin case was under his arm, for he had come down to play to Robin.

"Of course I shall be glad of your help," responded Twinkles heartily. "And it will do you good. You haven't many chances of real honest work."

Allister vaulted over the fence, astonishing Twinkles by his agility.

"I will make a bargain with you. I will pick if you will go on singing."

Then a sudden impulse came into Twinkles' head.

"I want some words made into a song. Could you do it for me? I'm longing to sing them. Now you get up into that tree and pick from the top bough. Here is a basket."

Allister promptly obeyed, and then Twinkles repeated one of Robin's latest productions.

It was the description of a wind on its way from the sea into the heart of a Somerset valley, and Allister listened in silence.

"Let me come down and play it to you."

"Finish the tree first."

"Then recite me more. Where did you get it from? It's stolen from me."

Twinkles repeated another poem. Allister's long legs scrambled down to the ground.

"That's also a theft," he said. "It's what I was playing the last time I was here."

"Well," said Twinkles, gravely, "they're Robin's. He put into poetry what you were playing, and I want you to get them printed for him."

"They aren't bad," said Allister, sitting down on the grass and resting his back against a tree. I'm going up to London next week with my mother. I mean to take her away for the winter to Italy."

Twinkles stood still, and dismay showed itself in her face.

Allister opened his violin case.

"Shall I give you a tune?"

"No," Twinkles said, laughing; "you bewitch with your music. You might set me dancing, and I have work to do. Don't be lazy. If you're going away so soon, I shall make all the use of you I can. Oh! it's horrid of you to take away Lady Eleanor! Muffet will be heart-broken. She has fallen in love with your mother. I believe she lives on her smiles and words from day to day."

"I wish someone would live on mine."

"They would have very poor food," retorted Twinkles, "because you hardly ever talk sense. Could you be sensible for a few moments now? We desperately want some kind editor to take Robin's poems and pay for them. Will you help us?"

"But are they his?" argued Allister. "Thought is the centre of words, the creator, I should say. They're my thoughts put into rhyme. Has he written anything that his own brain has conceived?"

Twinkles promptly repeated an entirely original poem of her brothers, which met with Allister's approval.

"Give me the bunch of his poetic fancies, and I'll see what I can do."

Twinkles rushed into the house and returned almost immediately with a roll of papers.

"I have copied them out, and you can have them, but you won't put them into your pocket and forget all about them, will you? And do be prompt, for we want money awfully badly."

Allister got up from his seat.

"If you won't let me play to you, I suppose I must go on picking apples. What a picturesque employment it is! But how deadly fatiguing!"

"Lazybones!" laughed Twinkles.

"Will you give me some tea after our work is over?"

"Yes, if you can stay. I know Robin will be disappointed if he misses you."

"It's all 'Robin,'" said Allister, looking at her gravely. "Is your life entirely merged into his?"

"Almost."

Twinkles' eyes grew soft and dreamy as she spoke.

"He is so brave and uncomplaining. As a little boy, he gloried in his heritage of suffering; but I think it has come to be harder now that he is a young man. He says it is only in dreams that he lives on his legs, like other people."

"It's hard luck on him, but the soul can enjoy much more than the body."

"Yes, that's what makes him so happy. I wish I had as happy a soul as Robin, but he always lives so close to heaven."

Allister looked at her with reverent eyes.

"Oh," he said with a sigh, "how good, how very good I should be if I lived with you and Robin! Couldn't we do it? Don't laugh at me. I've had my fling of sunshine and fun. I want a time of sweet, dreamy peace. I want love to come into my life. It has come already; could you care for a wandering fiddler, Twinkles? Could you marry me? I would not separate you from Robin. We should be a happy trio, we would go to the sunny south, or, if you elected to stay in grey England, I would find some sunnier, brighter nook than this, with an old garden, by a nightingale wood. And I would make music and Robin would make poems, and you would make a Paradise for us both!"

"You are stark, staring mad!"

It was not the usual response a girl makes to her first proposal, but Twinkles was dumfounded. Allister looked at her reproachfully.

He had been busily stripping a bough of apples as he talked, but now he came towards her.

"I fell in love with you the first day I saw you," he said, earnestly. "It is my way to hide my feelings. I never could express them. Of course I know my defects, but I could be clay in your hands. I have enough income to keep the three of us from starvation. It would be a simple, unpretentious life for all of us, but we would enjoy ourselves. And oh, my dearest, I would make you happy. I swear I would!"

Still Twinkles stared at him, not knowing whether to laugh or cry.

"If you're really in earnest," she said, "I'm very sorry that I can't fall in with your plans; I don't think you can really love me, Allister—not with the strong, deep, passionate, lasting love that I read about in books, and that I should have to have if I were to marry any one. You may think you like me now, but you'll forget me in a month's time. And we shouldn't be happy together. Don't look so miserable. What do you know about me? I have laughed and jested at and scolded you, in the fashion that Muffet has. And you have laughed and jested back. I don't know anything of your inner life or thoughts. You know nothing of mine. I am never going to marry, but if I did——"

"Well—if you did? Your soul is not awake yet, and I could wake it up if you let me. I know you are as pure and good and sweet as your life is, and as for me, I will make full confession at your feet of all that is in me. Thank God I have no skeleton locked up, nothing beyond youthful innocent follies to confess—nothing that would make you shrink from me. Tell me your idea of a husband—of the man you would choose above all others."

Twinkles stood leaning against an apple tree, her apples forgotten. She pushed back her sunbonnet and her merry face looked wistful and sweet.

"If I married," she said in a low voice, "my husband would have to be really good. He would have to love and serve God better than I do, so as to set me a good example. I know some women are so good in themselves that they make any man good who is with them, but I'm not like that. I always become like the people I live with. Robin helps me to be good; but I should expect my husband to do what he does. I shouldn't care about good looks. He must have nice, honest eyes, and he must be a worker in the world, not an idler. If he need not work to support himself he must work for others. I don't like idle men, I can't respect them. There is such a lot to be done in the world, and so few who will really give up their lives to do it!"

"Do you think me an idler? Is art nothing in your eyes? Is music to be laid aside, and all that makes the world beautiful, for the business house, and the sordid money making, and the labourer's tools?"

Twinkles shook her head impatiently.

"I don't care about beauty, if it is only on the surface."

"Oh, you are very young!" sighed Allister. "You are for strenuous toil and interfering philanthropy. You don't realise what it takes to make a world. There must be all sorts and conditions of needs. If my music inspires, comforts, cheers, is it idleness on my part to wander round and make music to the depressed and suffering ones? Take your brother, for instance."

"Yes," said Twinkles, quickly, "it is ungrateful of me, for you have done him good. And I am not blaming you for your vocation, I am only telling you the kind of ideal husband I have in mind. Of course, I shall never meet him and never marry; but I won't lower my ideal. I should need a strong man, a self-denying, noble worker, one of whom I could say, 'He is my husband! I am proud to belong to him.'"

Allister looked at her with a mixture of feelings. Annoyance, amusement, admiration, and bitter disappointment formed a part. Though he had not meant to speak definitely to Twinkles so soon, he believed himself seriously in love with her; it was a creed with him to adopt an easy, indifferent tone when he wanted to conceal his feelings, and it was natural that

Twinkles should not attach much importance to his proposal.

He said, now almost irritably,

"Yes, and those high, heroic sentiments have kept more women single than anything else. Why should you wait for an impossible hero only found in trashy books, and let the ordinary decent sort of chaps go by? You disdain my sort now."

"No, I don't indeed," said Twinkles, almost tearfully. "I like you extremely as a friend. Do stay at that. You and Robin and I are chums; let us stay so. Go to Italy with your mother, but don't forget us, and come back some day to charm us with your music."

"Do you want me to work or to idle?" he said, looking at her almost fiercely.

"Work, of course."

"Then I warn you, if I chuck my fiddle and turn into a money grubber, and a worker, I shall come back and *make* you marry me. You will be bound to do so, for you will have spoiled my life. I shall be a harassed, irritable man, a cynic, and I shall have a sour soul. All the sweetness and light in life will have gone from me. Take away my music and you will take away all incentive towards the high and heavenly attainments."

Twinkles looked frightened and bewildered.

"I don't want you to give up your music,"

she said. "I only suggest that you shouldn't idle. You know you idle through your days. You confess it yourself. I wish—I wish you would ask Muffet to be your wife instead of me. I am sure she would suit you better. She is strong. She could mould you. And I should love you to be my brother-in-law."

Allister gave a short laugh.

"You give me credit for very little feeling. You are the most extraordinary girl I have ever come across! You have said more insulting things to me this afternoon than I have ever been treated to in my life! You tell me my love is neither deep nor strong, nor lasting; that I will forget you in a month's time; that I'm an idler; and that your sister would suit me better. And this after I have offered you all that a man can offer!"

"Oh, I'm a wretch!" said Twinkles miserably; "but I cannot believe you are really in earnest. Now will you forget all about me, and will you, for Robin's sake, take these poems and get them printed? I feel you can if you will."

"I have said I will do what I can."

"There! I hear Robin's motor! Come in and play to us and be just our friend and nothing more. Will you carry my basket of apples for me?"

Allister stooped, and took up the baskets,

following Twinkles to the house without a word.

Muffet had returned, and was already in at the post-office, helping Kate to sort out the letters for the evening delivery. Robin had thrown himself down on his couch, with a sigh of fatigue. He looked up brightly, when they both entered the room.

"Oh! we've had a lovely time! the country has been heavenly! Have you been picking apples this whole afternoon, you poor creature? And has Allister been helping, or hindering?"

"Hindering, of course," said Twinkles laughing, but her laugh had a nervous ring in it.

"You have your fiddle, do give me a tune till tea is ready."

Robin's request was not denied.

Allister stood in his favourite corner, and shot an angry glance at Twinkles as she bustled to and fro with the tea things.

He considered she had mocked and made light of his proposal, and his music was consequently weird and passionate.

He did not always improvise, but he did so now, and Robin listened, expecting to be soothed.

His brows soon puckered, and he began to move restlessly upon his couch.

When, with a final crash and clash, the music ceased, Robin looked up.

"What's the matter with you? Why are you at such fever heat?"

"Ask your sister? She has treated me abominably. And I am out of tune with the whole world. No, I won't stay to tea; I couldn't. I never fail you, old chap, but, after all, it is women of my mother's age who bring repose and peace to one's spirit. I was a fool to think otherwise. Good-bye."

He took up his violin case and was off.

Robin lay still, and wondered. Twinkles did not enlighten him, but asked him about his ride, and talked volubly of her apples and all she meant to do with them.

A little later, Muffet returned from her rounds. As she sat drinking her cup of tea with great relish, she said:

"Lady Eleanor told me that her son is going to drag her abroad. I think it is a shame of him. She doesn't want to go, but she said so pathetically that he was her youngest son, and that she loved to think he wanted her with him. And she told me of a third son she has. He is a soldier out in India. I did not know there was another. I met Allister as I came home. He stopped and talked so strangely. Have you been quarrelling with him, Twinkles? He said, 'You will soon be relieved of my company, Miss Harcourt. I have escaped being shackled. Have you ever heard of fetters of love? They are faster than iron, but I am to be free—free as any bird on the wing. And as for your sister, she makes light of tremendous possibilities and realities, and goes on her way with a laugh in her eyes, and a dormant soul; nothing touches her, but her day will come. I am going to wait, and waiting twenty years will not tire me, for some natures develop and ripen later than others. And ripe fruit meets you half way, it is ready to drop into your hand. The sour undeveloped fruit resists.' There! that is word for word what he said! Is he half cracked?"

"Wholly so, I think," said Twinkles, humming a little song to herself. "Don't let us talk of him, Muffet. He is too old to alter. He will always be a pleasure-loving, pleasure-taking soul. To bask in the sun and make music to any and all who like to listen to him is all the aim and purpose he has. Sour, undeveloped fruit, indeed!"

And with a little grunt of disgust, Twinkles refused to talk about him any more.

CHAPTER X.

A SERIOUS TALK.

But when she went to bed that night, Twinkles could not sleep. She felt a longing to confide in some one. The old ache for her mother came back. Who but a mother could understand and comfort? Tears came into her eyes and ran down her cheeks, she buried her head in her pillow and sobbed aloud. And then a sudden impulse made her spring up and creep into Muffet's room. Muffet never failed anyone when they were in trouble.

Muffet was now combing out her long hair at the table; she was doing it in a leisurely manner, every now and then glancing at an open book which lay before her. Twinkles crept up and put her arms round her neck from behind. She saw the book was their mother's Bible.

"Don't look round, Muffet. I've been making an ass of myself; I want to tell you something. Do you know why Allister was so vexed?"

"I know it's something between you two," said Muffet, quietly.

"Yes, it is; I could not take him seriously,

could I, Muffet? He didn't do it at all in the proper way, only as if it was a kind of afterthought. And however he did it, my answer would have been the same."

"You don't mean to say," began Muffet, hesitating over putting her thought into words, "that——"

"Well, he asked me to marry him and come right away into Italy with him, and bring Robin with me. He had made a kind of little picture in his mind, I believe. It suddenly came to him that we would be a happy, light-hearted trio, singing and dancing and fiddling together; that's how we should go through life. There might be a house to shelter us, or there might not; there might be money for our needs, if not we would make some. He had enough to keep us from starvation. He would make music, Robin would make poems, and I a 'paradise' for them both. Yes, those were his identical words. Now, do you think that a proposal any girl would like to have?"

"Well, neither of us have had a proposal before, so we don't know much about it," said Muffet, in her frank, honest way. "Do you like him, Twinkles? That is the chief thing, I believe."

"Of course I like him—we all do; and I feel that Robin will be miserable if I have driven him away."

"You haven't; he made his plan to go."

"Yes; now does that look as if he is in earnest?"

"Do you really love him, Twinkles?"

"Of course I don't. I only like him because he makes me laugh, and cheers Robin up, and is a genius with his violin. I told him he was stark, staring mad!"

Twinkles laughed in a half shamed way, as Muffet turned round in astonishment; then the girls sat on a low couch together by the open window, and Twinkles went on talking:

"Yes, I know it was awful of me, and he is very angry, really angry with me. And now I'm wondering if I couldn't have been kinder, for it's good of him, I suppose, to ask me. I am not a beauty, am I, Muffet? And I have no money, and he was going to give a home to Robin, so that we should not have to part from each other."

"But if you don't want to marry him there is an end of it," said practical Muffet.

"You don't think I ought, as we are so poor?" faltered Twinkles. "But you see I don't know him well enough to trust him. Marriage is such an awful thing. You can do it in a hurry, but you can't undo it; and I feel he might get sick of me, and then we should all be miserable together, and I should have done Robin harm, not good."

"Don't think of Robin, think of yourself," said Muffet, a little impatiently.

"But it is Robin I am thinking of! How he would love to go to Italy! It would inspire him so! And then you wouldn't have to struggle with your accounts any more, Muffet! You would be able to live quite comfortably."

"What would be the good of that without you? Of course, I know you and Robin are all in all to each other, but I love Robin, and would be miserable without him. I would far rather have a struggle, all of us together, than be left alone to be comfortable. I know there is Poppet, but she seems settled for life where she is. Don't sacrifice yourself on my account, Twinkles, I beseech you. And I think those sacrifices in books are very silly and very wrong. There's only one thing ought to make you marry a man, and that is real love; if you don't love him don't marry."

"Oh, I'm so glad you think so," said Twinkles raising her head with a gesture of relief. "Then I certainly won't marry Allister. And when once he is away, we will forget all about him, won't we? You don't know how I've been thinking and thinking and getting quite homesick for mother. And Muffet, I feel that I could never marry any man who was not really good like mother and Robin. Don't you think I'm right?"

"I suppose so," said Muffet, slowly.

She kissed Twinkles before she went back to bed.

There was nothing small in Muffet's nature; though Robin had laughingly suggested that Allister admired her, there was not a trace of envy and jealousy in her heart when she knew that her sister was preferred before herself. When she was alone again, she sat on at her window and said regretfully to herself:

"If only Twinkles could have loved him, it would have brought us very close to Lady Eleanor. She might have been a second mother to us. But Twinkles does not love her as I do."

Allister did not come to the cottage again, but the day he was going away, a village boy appeared with a note for Twinkles, and said he was to take back an answer.

This was the note:

"My Dear Flouter,

I am going away, and you will be relieved, I am sure. But I am in dead earnest, and I do not mean to slip out of your life, so don't feel too secure in your maiden fortress. If you prefer earthen pitchers to Bohemian vases, don't complain if the Bohemian vase gets shattered in its struggles to metamorphose itself. I won't be treated unkindly by you, because I don't want you to have remorse later on. Send me a gentle word of farewell, and tell your scribbler that I won't forget him. After all, it is not a crime to ask for love in return for love.

Yours in reality,

ALLISTER BLAIR."

For a moment Twinkles felt inclined to ignore this effusion, then she carried it up to her room and wrote the following:

"DEAR MR. BLAIR,

Forgive me if I was unkind the other day. I did not mean to be. I think I ought to have thanked you for asking me to be your wife. But I have never been spoken to by anyone as you spoke to me, and I could only tell you straight out how I felt. I hope you will have a nice time abroad, and please let us know about Robin's poems soon. And believe me when I say, that you have been one of our nicest, pleasantest friends, and we want to consider you one still.

Yours very sincerely,

TWINKLES."

Allister nearly tore this into a thousand bits when he received it, then he smoothed it out and put it into his breast pocket.

"Ice pudding!" he muttered to himself; "sweet and cold and indigestible, but I'll wear it next my heart notwithstanding!"

Robin missed his musical friend; but he was enchanted one morning to hear again from the publisher who had taken his first story. He was ready for another now, for he wanted a serial for a new magazine he was starting. He gave him a very short time in which to do it. If Robin could not manage it so quickly, no other story would be required for another twelvemonth. Robin set to work at lightning speed. No one was to speak to him or interrupt him. For three or four days he worked at fever heat. Twinkles implored him to go more slowly, but he would not heed; and then came a day when back and head refused to work, and he lay prostrate in bed murmuring incoherently to himself.

Twinkles nursed him and comforted him.

"You will have to store up your strength a little more," she said; "you let it all out at one go, and then you collapse."

"I'm no good at all," moaned Robin. "I am only good for lying still and doing nothing."

"For lying still and suffering," corrected Twinkles. "Well, that is your heritage, is it not?"

Robin smiled radiantly. The mention of his heritage still brought light to his eyes and a glow in his heart.

"Yes," he said, "I've been taught that I can't have two heritages. I thought once that I might turn out a genius; but suffering is my heritage, and when I forget it I have a bout to make me remember it. I shall be only a scribbler. That is what Allister called me; but scribbling brings in money. I do want to be the bread-winner."

"And so you are, and so you will be. But you must go more slowly."

When his attack was over, Robin set to work again. One afternoon when there was an awful storm of rain and wind raging outside, Twinkles came into the kitchen very dolefully. Everything had gone wrong. It was drying day, and Mary could not hang the clothes out in the garden. It was bad for Robin to have them steaming in the kitchen, and the little back scullery was too small to hold them.

Muffet had such a bad cold that Twinkles advised her to go to bed and stay there. She intended taking the evening letters round herself. She had just been out in the back yard trying to clear the gutters that ran round the roof. The water was pouring into the back kitchen and now was coming down the open chimney in the front kitchen, with a hiss and roar that was quite deafening.

Twinkles shivered as she looked out of the window, then slipped off her wet shoes and stood them in the fender to dry. Drawing up a low stool in front of it, she sat down and stretched out her toes to warm. She glanced at Robin. He was writing with a rapt smile about his lips. She knew she ought not to interrupt him, and yet the longing to talk overcame her scruples.

"No one can be happy a day like this, can they, Robin?"

"Don't speak," murmured the boy; "it's delicious. 'The fringed palms were shading the young couple, as they sat watching the blue sea; and the golden light of the setting sun gilded the snow-white sails of their little boat in the harbour.'"

A smile curled about Twinkles' lips as she listened to him.

"I wish I could get away from the depressing wet day like Robin does," she muttered. "It's a blessed thing to have imagination."

Then she shut her eyes.

"Go on, Robin. I'm going to be there with you. I see the sun and the little boat, and the palms. Is she very beautiful?"

"She has a beautiful soul," said Robin writing away; "it is just now that Alick has come to the end of his wanderings. She has been waiting for him a whole year, and he finds her where he left her."

"But I hope she has been doing something

besides sitting by the sea and watching it," said Twinkles, with her sense of humour. "You mustn't let her form habits of idleness before she is married, Robin, or she will want to continue them afterward."

Robin stopped writing and threw his head back on his pillow.

"I'm afraid I am writing trash!" he said with his merry laugh. "I always mean to do better when I begin, but I drift into great nonsense. Miss Walpole would be shocked, but I cannot preach when I write. Do you think I ought to?"

Twinkles wrinkled her brow as she stared into the glowing fire and considered the matter.

"I suppose there must be writers to amuse people," she said slowly, "and to excite and exhilarate them. Then there are writers who stamp their books with nastiness, and morbidness and wretchedness; and then there are those who lift their readers towards heaven. I know I've read books that I shall never forget—they have helped me so."

Robin's pen dropped out of his fingers.

"My books will never help anyone," he said in a mournful tone.

"But they might," urged Twinkles. "You have always helped me to be good, Robin. You have taught me patience and resignation, when things go wrong; you have shown me how pain and suffering and difficulties only make our hearts the happier, when we open them to the Comforter. And there are lots of people who have the same heritage as you, and perhaps don't know how to bear it, and have never been taught the way."

Robin's bright eyes gazed thoughtfully at his sister.

"But I feel such a prig when I write about those things. I can only talk over them with you."

Twinkles was silent. She was anxious that Robin should do better work than he was doing. She felt he was too good to miss it. Presently she said slowly:

"I wonder if the blind and deaf and dumb people who were cured by our Saviour, felt prigs when they told others about the One who had healed them."

Robin lay back amongst his cushions very still. And then the clock struck five, and with a little sigh Twinkles slipped her shoes on again. She got up from the fire and faced Robin, with a swift change of subject.

"I tell you what Robin, Muffet is a trump! I'm simply wretched because I have to go out in this howling storm and deliver those letters! She goes twice a day in all weathers without a murmur."

"I wish you hadn't to go," said Robin.

"But I have. And I had better make the plunge at once."

She dashed out of the room and upstairs to get her hat and ulster. A few minutes after, she was bravely trudging on her round. Muffet's oilcloth cape and cap were on her, but the onslaught of the wind was so terrific when she left the shelter of the village, and began to mount a hill, that she could hardly keep her feet. Still she persevered; she delivered the post at the Hall, was glad that the absence of Lady Eleanor saved her the necessity of walking still further, and was crossing a bit of rough common on her way to Mrs. Damer's when a fresh burst of storm and wind broke full upon her. Her cape flew over her head and in her struggles to extricate herself, the strap of her post bag broke, and the wind whirled it away, dashing it into a pond that was close at hand. Twinkles gave a cry of despair, but without stopping to think, she waded bravely into the pond. At all cost she knew she ought to rescue that bag. Happily it was still afloat, for it was not very heavy. She gave another cry as the wind swept it still farther out of her reach and then an answering shout made her look up, and on the opposite side of the pond, she saw Gascoigne Damers.

"Go back, Miss Muffet!" he called out. "I'll get your bag. You're in a desperate plight."

Twinkles was only too glad to obey. In another moment he had joined her, bag in hand.

"I was coming to meet you. It's a scandalous shame you should be out such weather! Here's your wretched bag! It all comes of women trying to do men's work."

"I have no breath to argue!" gasped Twinkles. "To begin with, I'm not Muffet!"

He looked quite disappointed, then in an anxious tone he asked:

"Is she ill? Has anything happened?"

"She has a very bad cold, so I made her stop in bed."

"Look here, you let me take this bag for you, and go home and change; you must be wet through."

"Indeed I shan't! I mustn't let this bag go out of my hand."

"It has done that already," laughed Gascoigne. "Come, Miss Twinkles, don't be pig-headed, show more breadth of mind than your sister does, and let me help you."

"I'll tell Muffet you think her pig-headed and narrow-minded!"

"For heaven's sake don't! I admire her courage and pertinacity more than I can say. Come on, then, and I'll get my mother to lend you dry things."

"My dear Mr. Damers," said Twinkles, setting out at a brisk stride. "Don't you know

SHE GAVE ANOTHER CRY AS THE WIND SWEPT IT FARTHER OUT OF HER REACH (Page 149)

post-men and post-women are impervious to weather? When you had a post-man did you offer to give him a change of boots every time he got wet?"

"Girls have no business to do the work of men; they are not fitted for it."

"If we've heard that remark from your lips once, we've heard it a hundred times. I can't talk, it's too—too windy!"

It was, indeed, too stormy to hear each other speak. They both arrived at Mrs. Damers' cottage breathless.

"You must apologize to your mother for the newspaper being so wet," said Twinkles, as she stood in the porch and produced the post."

"Do come in!" pleaded Gascoigne.

"I can't really. I'm bound to deliver these within a certain time, and if I failed, Muffet would get into trouble. You wouldn't wish that, would you?"

"Have you any more to deliver?"

"Of course I have. The old Walpoles would make an awful fuss if they didn't get their papers up in time. Oh, how I hate you!—abominable, ungovernable wind!"

Her cape had whirled over her head again.

Gascoigne released her, and Twinkles' eyes and smile were merry as she departed.

"Now, I wonder how often he sets out to

meet Muffet?" she said to herself. "He was awfully disappointed this evening."

She reached the Walpoles without any more misadventures. Miss Walpole ran out into the hall to meet her.

"My dear child, what an awful evening for you to be out! Why, it is not Muffet?"

"No, it's I. Muffet has an awful cold and is in bed."

"Frances!" shouted a hasty voice; "have the newspapers come? Bring them in?"

"That's the Captain!" said Miss Walpole nervously. "Why, my dear, the papers are streaming!"

"Yes; they've been in a pond. I'm so sorry."

"Wait a minute; this is your last house, is it not? You must be dried a little before you go home. Have you been in the pond too?"

Without waiting for a reply, Miss Walpole bustled away with the papers. Twinkles heard the angry comments of the Captain and of his brothers about the condition of their post. Then Miss Walpole returned, and drew Twinkles into her cosy little sanctum. She had one room in the house free of tobacco smoke; and this was it, for her brothers never came inside it.

"Sit down by the fire, dear. Oh, what a state you are in! Wait a moment."

The good little woman bustled away, and

very soon appeared with a pair of stockings and serge skirt.

"Now slip into these—we are about the same height—and leave your wet things here. And I've ordered a hot cup of coffee for you. Oh, dear! I do wish I had the charge of you young people. You are so rash; you take no thought nor care of yourselves. I told your sister yesterday she was not fit to be out. In fact all this week she has been struggling against a cold."

"I wish we had you to look after us," said Twinkles, laughing. "But you see we are working girls—not fine ladies, and no one minds the weather if they have to earn their living."

"How is the dear boy?" asked Miss Walpole.

"I left him in the throes of his writing."

"Don't let him write rubbish," Miss Walpole said abruptly.

"How funny you should say that this evening! I was talking to him about it before I left. You know, when he was a tiny boy he used to ease his pain by inventing blood-curdling adventures; the more he suffered, the wilder were his flights of fancy! And I think it is something like that now. He can't trust himself to write anything pathetic or to mention pain and suffering—it comes home to him too much. He wants to get away from all physical weakness."

Miss Walpole nodded.

"I understand. I must come and see him to-morrow if I can. Do you want to go? Well, I won't keep you, for the sooner you are home the better. I do hope you won't be the worse for your wetting."

"Frances! Frances! You have moved my glasses. I left them on the mantelpiece. Confound it!"

The stentorian tones of General Walpole called his sister away. Twinkles had thoroughly enjoyed her cup of coffee. She lifted up her face to Miss Walpole and kissed her.

"Thank you ever so much for being so kind to me. Does no one ever look after you? You seem the one to do everything for everybody."

"I am a caretaker, dear," said Miss Walpole with a smile. "All women are, or ought to be if they aren't. Coming, Fred! Coming! Good-bye."

She ran out of the room with renewed cheerfulness and courage. Twinkles trudged home.

CHAPTER XI.

"I'VE BURNT MY TRASH!"

"Robin!"

There was no answer. The kitchen was very dark, for dusk had set in, the fire seemed nearly out. For a moment Twinkles' heart almost stood still, for she saw her brother was lying motionless on his couch. Softly, on tiptoe, she approached him. His eyes were closed, but there were recent tears on his cheeks. Twinkles had never remembered seeing Robin cry. If he shed tears, they were shed in the privacy of his bed room. Anxiously she put her hand on his forehead. With a little sigh, he looked up.

"Are you back, Twinkles! Oh, how wet you must be! The storm is terrific!"

"I'm all right, but why are you in such gloom? And what is the matter with the fire? It seems choked with rubbish. Why, Robin, it is burnt paper!"

She knelt down impulsively by his side and grasped his two hands, which were hot and feverish.

"Now, Cock Robin, what have you been doing? Tell me."

Robin lay back on his cushions looking at her in rather a tragic way.

"I've burnt my trash, Twinkles. God helping me, I am never going to write any more!"

Twinkles gave a little gasp.

"Not your story that you have been working so hard at for all these weeks? Why, Robin, you had nearly finished it!"

"All but three chapters."

"What made you do it? Oh, Robin dear, I'm so sorry! I'm afraid you took my words to heart. I never dreamt of your destroying the work of so many weeks."

Robin smiled at her, and it was his wonderfully radiant smile.

"It's been a battle, but I hope I've won. I have been lying here thinking it all out, and—and praying, Twinkles. I've told God if He has given me the gift of writing at all, He will help me to write something that He will not be ashamed of seeing. I don't see my way clear yet, but I believe God won't fail me. And I shall write something else to-morrow. I can't to-night. I'm rather—rather fagged—but I've burnt my boats, my paper, I should say. And I shall never go back, for I've made a kind of vow to-night, and I liked the dark, Twinkles—for, do you know—I really have heard God speaking to me!"

Twinkles bent her head over the couch and

kissed her brother warmly, but Robin felt a hot tear drop on his cheek.

"Oh, Robin, you are an angel! Much, much too good! I won't be sorry. I'm glad, for now you have bounded up miles above me, where you will stay, I know. God won't fail you, Robin. You'll write something that will live and last, something that will help others towards Heaven!"

It was always Twinkles' way to encourage her brother. If she felt frightened at his summary proceedings, she did not show she was, to him. And she saw that he was exhausted with the strain of his mental conflict. She slipped off her wet shoes and cape, and got some wood from the back kitchen. Very soon the flames were flickering cheerily up the chimney, and the lamp was lighted. She ran up to Muffet and found her comfortably asleep. Then she came back to Robin and began to get their evening meal ready. She wisely left the subject of his writing, and was making him laugh at her late experiences when Muffet called her.

"I'm awake, and am so dull. I hear you enjoying yourselves. Can't I come down?"

Twinkles flew up the little stairs. The kitchen was closed up for the night, and was now so bright and cheery that Muffet obtained her way. Wrapped in a very thick dressing gown, she came downstairs and with a rug round her, sat in an easy chair by the fire. Then Twinkles had to repeat her experiences and Muffet enjoyed them as much as Robin.

"I'm so glad it wasn't me," Muffet said. "I should hate to have Gascoigne find me in such a plight. He is dead against my being the postman. It's rather nasty of him, because he knows it adds to our income."

"I can't think how you can do it, Muffet," said Twinkles. "I should be dead sick of it before long, and now the winter is coming on with the rough weather and the dark nights and mornings, it really is not fit for you. I wish I could earn a little money; you see, we shall not have many visitors for teas now. That bit of trade has gone!"

Muffet nodded wisely.

"Yes, we can't afford to lose a penny. I don't mind my evening rounds at all. I enjoy coming home so, especially if it is wet and rough. I picture the scene to myself often, before I open the door—the firelight and Robin on his couch, and you getting the tea ready; and when there's a smell of baked apples or a hot cake it's quite delicious! The morning round is the most interesting, but I shall be able to start again to-morrow. I am tons better."

"Miss Walpole thinks that all women ought to be nothing but caretakers," said Twinkles, thoughtfully; she forgets so many have to earn their own living now."

"I suppose she thinks they ought to earn their living by caretaking," said Muffet. "That was the old-fashioned idea; if a poor lady wanted to work, she went as a governess or companion. Both are caretakers."

"And if they marry they are still caretakers," said Twinkles; "for I'm sure most men expect their wives to take care of them and make them comfortable."

"Gascoigne wouldn't," said Muffet; "he is too masterful! He considers men ought to be caretakers, not women. He hates a woman to lift up her little finger to help herself. I pity his wife when he gets one."

"I rather admire him for that, he is so courteous and chivalrous to women. He certainly is the caretaker in his family. Look how he watches over his mother!"

"Did you see her?" asked Muffet.

"No, I would not go in, though Gascoigne pleaded hard. I should like to have seen her. She hasn't been so well lately."

"I always think," said Muffet, thoughtfully, "that Gascoigne ought to have Lady Eleanor for his mother, and Allister have Mrs. Damers. Lady Eleanor would be so proud of Gascoigne, and he would look after her so beautifully! She deserves an attentive son."

"You are always thinking of your darling Lady Eleanor," laughed Twinkles. "I am sure Allister is very fond of his mother and very good to her. It would be rather fun to change some people's belongings, but I'm certain that neither Mrs. Damers nor Lady Eleanor would like to exchange their sons!"

Robin did not take part in this discussion, though he was listening to it. Muffet thought him singularly silent, but it was not till he had gone to bed that she was enlightened as to what had passed. She was dismayed when she heard it.

"I think it is an awful pity, Twinkles! I must say I'm thinking of the money part of it. Robin's writing has been liked, because he has such a sense of humour and fun, and such originality. He couldn't write pious, goody-goody stories. It will be a dead failure."

"No," said Twinkles with decision; "I don't agree with you. He can still write fiction, and bring as much humour into it as he likes, but he can bring high ideals into it as well. I don't believe his gift will be taken away from him because he wants to use it for God."

Muffet said no more. She often wished she had Twinkles' strong and cheery faith in God. If Muffet was the better of the two as far as physical build and strength went, Twinkles had more mental and spiritual power.

When the next day dawned, Robin faced it with a little of his old buoyancy. He had not slept well, but he had in his wakeful hours caught a glimpse of what he might portray. It was a passing vision of a character that might be very human and winning, and yet be the personification of God's possibilities overruling man's impossibilities.

"Out of weakness made strong." He was eager and anxious to begin upon it; and directly he was settled on his couch, Twinkles brought him his writing board and stylo pen.

"There you are, Cock Robin!" she said, merrily. "Good luck to you! You always say you find the beginning of a story easier than the end, so I don't believe you'll have much difficulty this morning. Scribble away, and if you want anything, sing out for me. It's a sunny morning, and like the maid in our nursery rhyme, I shall be in the garden hanging out the clothes."

"I shall manage first rate," responded Robin with shining eyes. And for the whole of that morning his pen and brain were busy. Twinkles peeped in once or twice, but she made herself scarce, for she knew that he wrote better when quite alone.

It was hard work for Robin in the ensuing days. He strove to make up for lost time, and worked as usual with more zeal than discretion.

Then came two bad days of fever and pain, when he had to go to bed and stay there, but at the earliest opportunity he was at it again, and his sisters watched him with admiring, yet anxious eyes.

As the time drew near when the copy had to be delivered, Twinkles grew more and more nervous.

Robin was putting his whole soul into this book. His face was getting quite transparent; he lost his appetite, he was feverishly restless unless he was writing, and his eyes seemed to grow more and more languorous and large.

"He is using himself up," Twinkles confided to Muffet. "What ought we to do? It will break his heart if he doesn't finish it, but he is making himself ill!"

"We must let him finish it if he can!"

And there seemed doubt when the last day came whether he could. He woke with a splitting headache. Twinkles took him a strong cup of coffee.

"Look here," she suggested; "let me write to your editor and send him what you have written. The last chapter can wait. Don't you write a word to-day. You are not fit for it."

"I couldn't fail him. I must finish it. It is all in my head."

"Then don't trouble to get up. You are only fit for bed."

But Robin struggled up; and Twinkles wisely remonstrated no more.

He laboured on manfully all the morning, with flushed face and heavy eyes. In the afternoon he was at it again, revising, correcting and finishing. Twinkles had followed his story chapter by chapter; she had laughed and cried over it, and criticised unsparingly. Now she was infinitely relieved that his work was on the eve of being finished.

And then about three o'clock in the afternoon, in sailed Mrs. Handley, prepared for a long stay and talk, and Bumbles was with her She had been very kind and really interested in them all, and when she could spare the time, felt it her duty to go and see how they were getting on.

Robin groaned when he saw her coming.

"What can I do? I haven't finished."

"Leave the room and write in your bedroom," said practical Muffet, who was renovating one of her serge skirts on the kitchen table.

Bumbles flung himself on Robin's couch.

"I haven't seen you for years. Keep me to tea, and tell me a story," he whispered.

Poor Robin shook his head despairingly, and Mrs. Handley, looking across at him, was at once really concerned about his health.

"Your brother is looking very ill," she said to Muffet quietly. "He is getting much thinner."

"Robin has one of his bad headaches to-day," Muffet replied quickly. "Will you excuse him if he leaves us? He isn't up to talking, and he has work on hand that must be finished to-day."

"Come and see me another day," said Robin, turning to the disappointed Bumbles. And then, with a little apology to the rector's wife, he left the room.

Twinkles ran after him, to make him comfortable. When she came back, Mrs. Handley said:—

"Your brother is fortunate in having such attentive sisters, but, my dears, he looks to me in a high fever. Do you ever take his temperature?"

"Yes," Twinkles said, "often. He always has a high temperature, when he gets these attacks. But there's nothing to be done. He just has to bear the pain till it leaves him. We hoped he would outgrow his weakness, but he is more delicate now than when he was a little boy. He cannot get about so actively as he used to do."

"What a suffering life for such a handsome boy!" said Mrs. Handley, pityingly. "I wonder he is as bright as he is."

"It is his heritage," Twinkles said, "and he glories in it!"

Mrs. Handley looked at her quite uncomprehendingly. Then Twinkles tried to enlighten her, and she listened with interest.

She did not stay so long as usual, and for the first time the girls were glad to see her go.

Then ensued a busy time packing up the precious MS. and posting it.

Robin went promptly to bed, and was in it for nearly a week from overstrain.

He anxiously watched every post. Muffet said to Twinkles once when she had just come out of his room,

"I hope mother is not able to see Robin now. She would be so distressed. I am not sure whether this writing will be able to go on. It oughtn't to do so, if it will shorten his life."

"Oh," gasped Twinkles. "Don't say such things! This last story is an exception. He had so little time in which to write it, and it taxed his emotion so! I think he has surpassed himself. I am longing to hear what is thought of it; of course, it is the suspense that is so trying to Robin!"

But the suspense came to an end at last. The letter came, and Robin tore it open breathlessly, then his face paled. He held it out to Twinkles.

"It is refused. Read what he says. He is sending it back to me by the next post."

Muffet and Twinkles were stricken dumb by this climax. The publisher wrote very politely, saying he saw there was good stuff in it, and that it might possibly suit some other publisher, but that his magazine required a different style of writing, and he had expected something on the same lines as he had received before. As the time had gone, he would require nothing else for the immediate present; but that he would still leave his offer open for another year, if Robin could write something in his previous style.

Twinkles did not know what to say. Muffet was the one who spoke. "You must write as you did before, Robin. Never mind; we must do without the extra money."

"I never mean to write as I wrote before," said Robin, throwing his head back on his pillow with his "war horse snort," as Twinkles called it.

There was silence.

"If we starve, I shan't," said Robin, facing his sisters almost defiantly.

Muffet said no more, and soon went out into the orchard to look after her fowls.

Twinkles sat down by the fire with her mending basket. She was not going to leave Robin to bear this blow alone.

Presently Robin heaved a sigh.

"It seems as if my vow and purpose has been a failure, Twinkles."

"No, it hasn't," the girl said quickly. "It is rather a test of faith, isn't it? But it's all right, Robin, it must be. We will try another publisher, one who likes religious stories."

"I needn't have worked at such a rate," lamented Robin.

"No, but you see we could not tell that he would not like it."

And when the rejected MS. came back, Twinkles packed it up and sent it off by the very next post to another publisher.

It was while he was waiting for news of it that Robin received another communication.

And if bitter disappointment had been his portion before, he was rewarded now.

A cheque for £20 was enclosed by an editor of a very good class magazine, saying he was making use of several of his poems, and would like to see more work of his.

Robin was astounded.

"I have never sent him any of my poems. How has he got hold of them?"

Twinkles confessed what she had done.

"I was afraid Allister had forgotten. I did not like to raise your hopes. Isn't it splendid, Robin? We need not have feared."

"I have spent some uncomfortable nights,"

Robin said. "Things always appear worse at night, don't they? And my poems aren't rubbish then, Twinkles! I was afraid you thought they were. I wonder where Allister is now? I should like him to know they're a success, for it was his music which inspired me."

"It is a pity his music doesn't inspire himself," said Twinkles, a little severely.

Robin looked at her and laughed.

"You're always down on that fellow. I like him. I hope we'll see him again one day."

But Twinkles would not echo this hope.

CHAPTER XII.

GASCOIGNE'S MOTHER.

Success was always good for Robin. His face seemed to fill out, and his health improve from the time he got that cheque. Twinkles and he kept the cottage atmosphere bright with their fun and laughter through all the dreary, dark November days. Gascoigne loved to drop in upon them in the afternoons on his way home from his school, and they all treated him as one of themselves.

One afternoon he approached with a very grave face.

"What is the matter?" asked Twinkles. "Have you been flogging a boy?"

He shook his head.

"My mother is very bad; and I've been having a long talk with her doctor. I have just been making up my mind to give up the school."

Muffet looked at him gravely.

"I was afraid you would do that," she said; "but is it necessary? You have a very trustworthy maid, and you could get a trained nurse to help her! Surely a man need not turn himself into a sick nurse."

"My mother wants me to be more with her. She frets when I am away."

"But she wouldn't want to keep you by her side all day long?" Twinkles remarked.

"Yes, she does," said Robin with conviction; "and you must do it, Damers; I would if I were in your shoes."

Gascoigne smiled at Robin's eager tone.

"I won't fail her," he said with a little nod. "But you won't see much of me now."

"Is she very ill?" Muffet asked, softly.

"The doctor says it is a question of only a few months," he responded quietly. The shadow of death seemed to have suddenly crept into that cheerful kitchen. They sat silent. Their recent loss made their hearts ache, for the one who would be so soon bereft, even as they were.

When Gascoigne rose to go, Muffet accompanied him to the door.

"I am so sorry for you," she said.

He took her hand in his.

"Give me a word of comfort, Miss Muffet. You are so brave and courageous! How can I break it to her? I feel I ought to do so. She clings so to life, poor little thing! How shall I be able to face death with her and keep her brave and smiling through these dark months ahead of us?"

Muffet's cheeks paled.

"I am not good," she faltered; "I wish I were. But Robin is. Would Mrs. Damers ever care to see him! He knows about pain and suffering. It is his heritage. And he has a strong faith in God."

"Yes," said Gascoigne, with deep feeling; "I know he has; and he isn't ashamed of it. I don't know why we should be. But I'd like you to help her. Women understand women. Will you come and see her to-morrow?"

"I will, certainly, if she would like to see me," said Muffet.

"Thank you. I felt I could turn to you."

And he went out of the door, and down the street without another word.

Muffet stood looking after him with scared eyes. Then she went back into the kitchen. Robin was alone, for Twinkles was busy in the back kitchen. She sat down by the fire, and presently looked across at her brother.

"I've been asked to help Mrs. Damers. How can I help her, Robin?"

"Did Damers ask you? I suppose he meant he wanted you to comfort her."

"How can I comfort her, when she is going to die? If I knew I was going to die, nothing would comfort me. I don't like to think of illness or death, I try to put them from me. They're horrible things; I don't like to read of them or think of them."

"Oh!" said Robin, with shining eyes; "they're so lovely to me. At least, I suppose the details of death will always be ghastly, but it is only in the transition. When you think of *afterwards!*"

"That's just it. The 'afterwards' is so uncertain."

"Oh, never, Muffet! I have often said to myself, 'We *know*—it isn't we *think,* or we *believe,* or we *hope,* or *expect,* but—we *know* that if our earthly house of this tabernacle were dissolved, we have a building of God, an house not made with hands eternal in the heavens!' "

"I wish I could feel sure like you do, Robin. I don't think I am in the circle of God's children at all."

It was so seldom that Muffet talked of religious things in any shape or form, that Robin had little idea of what her real feelings were. But he had tact enough to refrain from showing his surprise.

"But it is always easy to get inside," he said.

"How?"

"Isn't Christ the door? He said He was. I was just thinking of poor Mrs. Damers. It is such a comfort that it is all made easy for us, that the way is open, and we have only to come. Oh, Muffet, you can help her! If she hasn't read her Bible much, you can read it to her now."

"Yes, I could do that," said Muffet, slowly, "if she will let me, but it takes courage to read the Bible to a fashionable woman like Mrs. Damers. She would think it so funny of me."

"I shouldn't mind a bit."

"No, I don't believe you would, but I do. And I shouldn't know what part to read to her—Genesis or Revelations."

"Neither," said Robin, with a little laugh. "You had better read her something from the Gospels—it will come to you—or say her a verse, Muffet!"

"I don't think I know any. I might learn that one you quoted just now."

"Or a simpler one. Read her the 10th chapter of St. John, and say over and over that verse beginning 'I am the door.' But you really can't arrange beforehand. It depends upon what she says to you."

"It ought to be you to go and see her," said Muffet with grave conviction. "It's stupid of Gascoigne. He seems to think I am quite different from what I am, and he won't take 'no'."

"He thinks a lot of you, and the best of you," said Robin.

A flush came into Muffet's cheeks. She did

not deny her brother's assertion; for she knew it was true.

"There's no best about me," she said rather miserably. "When it comes to this kind of thing, I feel what a fraud I am. But I'll do my best to-morrow. Only I expect we shall talk about the fashions and Mrs. Blair's horrid little ways. Mrs. Damers and she hate each other, and if Mrs. Damers won't get on serious subjects, I can't force it."

"No, I should pray for her all the time, Muffet."

"I shall have more need to pray for myself," was the quick response.

There was no more serious talk, for Twinkles came dashing in.

"Now, lazy bones!" she said, addressing Muffet, "you might come and help me! I'm trying to mash potatoes and cabbage together to make a little hot dish for supper, and they refuse to mix! Will butter make them stick, do you think? I want to make them into balls, and fry them. Must I put an egg? And do you think a sprinkling of cheese would give a nice flavour?"

Muffet sprang up at once; and she did not touch upon her forthcoming visit to Mrs. Damers again. The next afternoon, in great fear and trepidation, she walked over to see Mrs. Damers. She was surprised to find her on her couch in the drawing room as usual; but she could not help noticing the blue drawn lines about her face. Mrs. Damers was always daintily dressed, and she still disdained caps, and wore her grey hair wonderfully curled and waved all over her head. She was in a mauve satin tea gown, and her fingers and wrists were covered with rings and bracelets. She welcomed Muffet kindly, but she was not her favourite, and Muffet knew it. Twinkles got on better with Mrs. Damers. She would chatter and laugh to her, as Muffet never could. The knowledge that Gascoigne expected her to help his mother at this juncture, made Muffet all the more constrained in speech. She talked of the weather, and of the country and of everything but of the one subject that was in her thoughts.

At last there was a pause, and then Muffet said very gently,

"I am so sorry you have not been so well."

A hard look came into Mrs. Damers' face.

"Oh, I am much the same, thank you. This country doctor has been frightening my son; but I have no faith in him."

Muffet did not know what to say. And then, as she looked up, she caught a rather frightened look in Mrs. Damers' eyes. She knew then that she was concealing her fears.

"Perhaps you ought to see a London doctor," Muffet said diffidently.

"I shouldn't think of it. They are all humbugs!"

There was a little silence, then Mrs. Damers gave a forced laugh.

"Gascoigne, poor boy! imagines that I am in a very bad way. He has given up his school, but I am thankful for that. I always hated him doing it. It was not the sort of work for him at all. And I shall be very glad to have him at home. It is dull for me, when I am left alone."

"Yes, I am sure you ought to have company," said Muffet eagerly. "One can bear things so much more easily, if one has someone to talk to."

" 'Bearing,' as you term it, has not entered into your life as yet, has it?"

"Not into mine, perhaps; but Robin has always been an invalid, and when he is in great pain, we like to be near him. He gets rather down if he is alone."

"I thought he was a bit of perfection!" Mrs. Damers said. "I heard he was never cross, never impatient—a boy saint, who gloried in his pains!"

"That isn't quite Robin," said Muffet, laughing. "But he is wonderfully happy, for he does suffer a lot."

"What makes him happy?"

Muffet's opportunity had come. Yet her cheeks were hot and scarlet as she said,

"Mother taught him how to be happy when he was quite a little boy. He has such strong faith in God that he takes his suffering as a heritage and life work, given to him that he may bear it for God. And hope about his future makes him happy."

"Does it? I hate that word future. I dread mine." She spoke quite naturally.

And then Muffet said rather shyly,

"But you need not, Mrs. Damers. Robin believes it will be the best time in our lives when we leave this world."

Mrs. Damers drew in a quick, short breath. Then she laid her hand impressively upon Muffet's arm.

"My dear child, I would give all I have to be possessed of that happy faith. Do you know that my son has broken to me my fate? Only another month or two to be in this world! Isn't it awful? It is a nightmare to me! Night and day I am trying to get away from the thought of it. And I have to eat and drink and sleep as if nothing had happened. It will send me mad!"

"It must be dreadful!" said Muffet, with grave emphasis. "I wish Robin were here. Would you like to see him one afternoon?"

"He wouldn't preach to me? I couldn't stand that!"

"No, no, Robin isn't a bit like that, but ——"

"Well, now, if you were in my place, what would you feel like?" said Mrs. Damers, looking straight into Muffet's eyes as she spoke; "I'd just as soon talk to you as to Robin."

"I'm not—not as good as I ought to be," faltered Muffet. "I'm afraid I should feel like you, but I do believe in God and Heaven, don't you? And in Jesus Christ. I think I should get hold of the Bible and find out where I was."

Mrs. Damers gave an impatient sigh.

"There's a Bible on that table. I believe Gascoigne thinks I ought to be reading the Bible, and nothing else. He put it there when I was not looking. Dying people are always supposed to read their Bibles, but I really should be bored to death if I did."

Muffet was silent.

"What good will a dry old book like that do me?" Mrs. Damers demanded impatiently; "I should want a clergyman to explain it to me, and I have told Gascoigne that I will not have Mr. Handley near me. I am not bad enough yet in health for him. Why, some parts of the day I feel quite well! And doctors are mistaken."

"I believe the Bible would make you happy," persisted Muffet. "May I say one verse in it that Robin said to me: 'For we know that if our earthly house of this tabernacle were dissolved, we have a building of God, an house not made with hands, eternal in the heavens.'"

"I don't know it," said Mrs. Damers, looking at Muffet with curious interest. "I am not a very religious person, or a good churchwoman. I should want to have that explained."

Muffet sighed.

"I am afraid I am no good at all," she said; "but would you like me to read you something simpler in it?"

"You can if you like, but I'm sure I shan't be interested."

Muffet took up the Bible and promptly turned to the tenth chapter of St. John. She read it slowly down till she came to the verse:—

"I am the door, by Me if any man enter in, he shall be saved, and shall go in and out and find pasture."

Then she said, "That's the verse which Robin says will show us how to be happy."

"Go on," said Mrs. Damers; "you have a soft voice, my dear; perhaps you will read me to sleep."

So Muffet read steadily on; and though Mrs. Damers was closing her eyes, she was listening hungrily to the words of life. When the following verses were read, she stopped her:—

"But ye believe not, because ye are not of My sheep, as I said unto you,

"My sheep hear My voice and I know them and they follow Me. And I give unto them eternal life and they shall never perish, neither shall any man pluck them out of My hand."

"That will do, my dear. Those verses have nothing to do with me. They are very soothing no doubt to the good people; but I don't believe, or hear, or follow! You might leave a marker in it, and put the book back. Have you heard whether Lady Blair will be home soon?"

It was of no use, Muffet thought, despondently; Mrs. Damers could not understand, and she could not explain; and desultory gossip occupied the rest of the time she was with her. She was very silent when she got home, and when she went to bed she studied her mother's Bible diligently. She never omitted her prayer and daily reading; but it was a duty and not a pleasure to her.

The following morning, as she was delivering the letters at Mrs. Damer's cottage, Gascoigne came out to her.

"I can't thank you enough for your visit yesterday," he said, eagerly. "You did my mother such a lot of good! She wants you to come again soon."

"But I did nothing," was Muffet's astonished reply. "It was a case of the blind leading the blind!"

"You managed to hit upon a subject that interested my mother," Gascoigne said. "She has actually insisted upon my reading to her this morning, and told me I was to read all I could find about sheep in the Bible. It was rather a tall order! She said she wanted to see how the metaphor was carried out."

"I wish I could have helped her," said Muffet wistfully, all her usual self-confidence dying away. "I do feel so sorry for her and for you."

"Thank you. I know you do. My poor little mother!"

He turned back to the house, with a sob in his throat.

And Muffet went on her way, blinded with tears.

But that night she, too, began studying the subject of sheep, and learnt several verses off by heart, for a future occasion.

About a week later, Gascoigne came into the cottage asking for Muffet.

Twinkles was ironing at the kitchen table.

"She has gone to Mortonbury to sell some eggs. She drove in Kate's cousin's cart; he is not coming back till just before post time. It is a chance for her to get the drive both ways."

Gascoigne looked worried.

"Won't she have done her business by this time?" he asked.

"I suppose she will, but she can't come back before John White is ready?"

"My mother has had one of her bad attacks this morning, and since she has come round she keeps asking for Miss Muffet. Do you think she would drive out with me, if I went in and fetched her?"

Twinkles looked at him with mischievous eyes.

"She might prefer John's company to yours."

Then her face softened at the remembrance of his mother's illness.

"If your mother wants her, of course she would go. Have you the trap outside?"

"Yes, I've just come to the post with a parcel I wanted to send away. I wonder that your sister drives about with farmers. It is not the thing for her to do. If I were her brother, I should not allow it."

Robin looked up from his writing.

"My dear chap, Muffet's brother is too wise to attempt to manage her! We like a life of peace, so we each go our own way."

"If you scold Muffet, you won't get her to come with you," Twinkles said.

Gascoigne strode to the door, and shut it with a bang.

The next moment they heard his horse clattering down the cobbled street.

"You and I are nowhere, Robin, are we?" laughed Twinkles. "I'm afraid Gascoigne will be rather a tyrant when he gets a wife."

Gascoigne found Muffet gazing into a shop window, in the high street of Mortonbury.

He got down, and put his case hastily before her.

She was perfectly ready to go with him at once.

"I must just find John White, and tell him I am not returning with him. I think he is in the 'Black Feathers.'"

"Jump up into the trap; my boy will hold the horse. I'll see this farmer. You can hardly go into the inn to look for him."

For once Muffet did not dispute him.

"Bring him out to me. I must thank him."

This Gascoigne did not do. He took the message, sprang up into the trap, and drove out of the town at a rapid rate.

"My mother keeps asking for you," he said.

"Your mother never used to care about me," said Muffet, thoughtfully.

"Oh, yes, she liked you all; but she seems to lean on you now. She's frightened, poor little dear! And I don't wonder. It's a cold-blooded way of meeting death!"

"I'm not the person to go to her, if she wants

to talk about good things," said Muffet, rather sorrowfully.

"She seems to think you are. She won't have anyone who preaches, or tells her that she is a wicked sinner, she says. Do comfort her if you can. I was up all night with her, and she really seems scared out of her wits. You see, her life hangs upon a thread in these attacks, and her brain is so clear that it makes it doubly trying."

"It is awful for her," said Muffet with emphasis.

"A man can't do anything," he said slowly.

"She implored me to stay with her; as if my presence would keep death at bay!"

Then they drove on silently, and soon came to the pretty little cottage, now in the valley of the shadow of death.

Muffet went into the bed-room with a strange sinking of heart. Mrs. Damers was in bed. Her features looked pinched and drawn, but she smiled at her when she saw her, and Gascoigne left them alone together.

"I wanted to see you," Mrs. Damers said in a hoarse whisper. "My boy is always talking of you. Will you try to comfort him when I am gone?"

This was so unlike what Muffet had expected that she could not answer for a moment. Never had she heard Mrs. Damers express any thought for her son. She was always entirely wrapped up in herself and her health.

"I don't expect I can," she faltered.

"Promise me you will try."

"If—if he wants me to, I will."

Mrs. Damers sank back on her pillows as if relieved.

"A good son makes a good husband," she murmured.

Muffet felt her cheeks get scarlet. Then she met Mrs. Damer's anxious eyes turned upon her.

"How can I get into the sheep fold?" she asked. "Do you think I might put myself in the class of 'any man'? And if so, what have I to do to get in at the door?"

"Nothing, I expect," said Muffet; "just come."

"'Come'? I don't understand that word. What is it to come?"

"I think you could ask Christ to take you," said Muffet, considering, for her study for many nights had not been in vain. She went on: 'I came across this verse, 'All we like sheep have gone astray and the Lord hath laid on Him the iniquity of us all.' Christ says He is the Good Shepherd, and he gave His life for us. Our sins were laid on Him when He died, so that makes us free from punishment, doesn't it?"

" I never knew I had any sins, " moaned Mrs. Damers. " I have always thought it was only dissenters and people in quite a low class of life who talked about their sins. I thought I had been a very good mother, and I've always kept within my income, and gone to church when I felt strong enough. But last night I had a nightmare about it—and—and it has hardly left me yet! I suppose from God's point of view, I haven't been quite what I ought to be."

" None of us have," said Muffet.

" I suppose not. But I am too tired to think about it. I feel I'd give anything to creep into —well, into His arms—and rest."

" Tell Him so," said Muffet softly. " I'm sure He is here, and will take you."

There was a dead silence in that room. The powers of evil were kept at bay, whilst a weary, untaught, unenlightened soul was taken into the loving, tender Arms of the Good Shepherd who had given His life for her.

There were tears in Mrs. Damer's eyes when Muffet looked at her.

" Leave me," she said. " I want to be with Him alone. I do believe He has done it."

And Muffet went, feeling how little she had helped, and yet how much was taking place.

CHAPTER XIII.

THE OLD, OLD STORY.

Christmas came, and with it came Poppet. She had a fortnight's holiday, and was determined to enjoy herself. She arrived home with presents for every one, and found Twinkles and Muffet deep in the mysteries of making a plum pudding, for they intended to enjoy their Christmas in common with others. Just before Christmas, Muffet heard from their Aunt Connie, and she enclosed a cheque for ten pounds as a Xmas gift amongst them all. This eased matters all round. Muffet threw off her anxious momentary cares; and was almost as light-hearted as Twinkles. But through all their merry talk and laughter, the thought of Gascoigne tending his sick mother by day and night obtruded itself into her thoughts. He had shouldered his burden cheerfully and bravely, and courted no pity from any one; but there was a softer, tenderer tone in his intercourse with others, especially with Muffet.

In the afternoon of Christmas Eve, Miss Walpole looked in. The little kitchen was bright and gay, and she smiled as she found herself surrounded by four eager young people, all talking hard.

"You make me wish I were young again," she said as she took a seat by Robin's couch. "How true it is that it is company and not comforts that makes for happiness!"

"We have both," said Robin gaily.

"And so have I, perhaps you think. But we are old and our bodies are making themselves felt. I have got the General in bed with bronchitis, and the Major is suffering from an attack of gout, and the Captain is writing furious letters to the *Times* about the incompetence of the Territorials. They are each shut up in their respective rooms, and have asked to be left undisturbed."

"Then that leaves you free," said Twinkles, stopping in her work of decorating the walls of the kitchen with holly. She and Poppet had been plundering some woods earlier in the day.

"Why don't you run away from those cross old men?" Twinkles pursued. "I should if I were you. I have told Robin that when he turns into a cross old Tartar, I will leave him."

"But you wouldn't do it, however cross and old he became," said Miss Walpole. "We can't run away from the corners in which we have been placed. And old age with its aches and pains is hard to bear. And it must come to us all."

Twinkles looked sober; then Miss Walpole asked about Robin's writing. He told her in bated breath of the change he had made in his style.

"I am not sorry a bit," he said. "But at present my book has not been a success. We are waiting to hear from another publisher now. If he declines it, I shall give up hope."

Miss Walpole's eyes were almost as bright as Robin's.

"Good boy! I always felt you could do better. You will make your way. You are bound to do so, and if you have to wait a little, it won't hurt you. I long to read your book."

"It nearly made him ill doing it," said Twinkles. "I am sure it has taken a year's strength out of him."

Miss Walpole did not stay long.

"I am really on my way to the Hall; but I could not resist the temptation of popping in amongst you for a few moments. I am going to ask after the Squire. I hear he is in London ill, and they expect him back to-day."

"Yes," said Muffet, turning round. "He has pleurisy, and they wired for Mrs. Blair this morning, but he is too ill to move at present. It will be a sad Christmas for the children left here alone."

"What a lot of illness we seem to have about just now! Poor Mrs. Damers is sinking fast,

I hear. Her devoted son nurses her night and day. It will be a sad Christmas for him."

Muffet's face sobered; and when a little later Miss Walpole left, she accompanied her to the door.

"If you wait a moment, I could take you to the Hall in Robin's motor. I am using it now. It is such a help for my Xmas parcels. Of course the petrol is expensive—for us at least —but Robin urged me to use it. I am just going with the post now."

"Oh," cried Miss Walpole in alarm, "I couldn't really, my dear; I couldn't trust myself to you! A friend of the Captain's told me as a positive fact that every one who drives a motor takes his life in his hand. I am frightened for you, but ten thousand times more frightened for myself."

She nodded a good-bye, and walked off. Muffet went into the post-office to collect her letters and papers. She did not take long to motor round to the various houses, though she had a few additional parcels to deliver at some farm houses that did not generally come within her beat. Lilac Cottage, Mrs. Damer's house, was reached in due time. It was a dark night and very cold. As she stood at the door, letters in hand, it was suddenly opened, and Gascoigne appeared. He stood looking at her in a dazed fashion for a moment, then said briefly:

"I thought it was you! And I wanted to tell you myself. Mother died at three o'clock this afternoon."

"Oh!" gasped Muffet in consternation. "I had no idea she was so ill! Oh, I'm sorry for you!"

Tears were in her eyes.

"Did she suffer much? I expect you can't talk about it."

"I'll walk down to the gate with you. I can hardly realise it yet, but I would like to tell you."

As they paced the gravel drive outside the house, he said quickly, "She knew she was going, this morning. She told me that I had had my last night watch with her, but I did not take it in. She had had a little beeftea—just a spoonful—and she lay down and asked me to read her the twenty-third Psalm, and she repeated every verse after me in a whisper. When she got to the verse, 'Yea, though I walk through the valley of the shadow of death I will fear no evil, for Thou art with me,' she stopped me and made me repeat the verse again. Then she murmured quite audibly, 'I believe it. Thou art with me,' and those were her last words. She seemed to sink into unconsciousness and we could not rouse her."

"Oh," said Muffet with a sob, "that was beautiful. She had no fear."

"No, none whatever," he replied. "She smiled radiantly after she spoke, and put her head down on her pillow like a tired child. I can't thank you enough for what you have done for her."

"I have done nothing," said Muffet, choking a little over her words. "Oh, Mr. Damers, it does seem such a sad time for her to be taken from you on Christmas Eve!"

"Well, she will have a happy Christmas," said Gascoigne. "I do believe that, with all my heart. She has drawn me very close to the unseen world. Good-night."

They parted, and Muffet came home to tell the sad news. Quiet fell upon them all, for Gascoigne was too much of a friend to be absent from their thoughts at such a time; and their Christmas day was shadowed with his loss.

And then only three or four days later another blow fell upon the village. Mr. Blair, the Squire, died in London. It was such a sudden illness that at first people could not take it in.

And, of course, it occasioned a good deal of talk and conjecture. He had not been very popular; his wife was heartily disliked, as she could not stand the country, or the country people, and would never take the slightest interest in any of them.

"Who will have the Hall now?" asked Robin, when he and his sisters were talking it over together. "Will Mrs. Blair have to turn out? Does it belong to her and her children?"

"No," said Twinkles; "Mrs. Handley says not. You see, her children are all girls; there is no boy."

"Then perhaps Mr. Allister will be the Squire," said Poppet.

"No, he is the youngest son; there's a Colonel Blair in India. He is the next heir, Mrs. Handley says."

"Anyhow, this will bring back Lady Eleanor," said Poppet. "And perhaps she will go back to reign at the Hall if Colonel Blair is a bachelor."

Muffet's face lightened.

"Oh, I hope she will! That horrid Mrs. Blair has snubbed her so. It will serve her right if she has to turn out, and give way to Lady Eleanor."

"What a lot of changes have taken place since we came here! Gascoigne Damers will leave us now, I suppose. There is nothing to keep him here."

Poppet spoke carelessly. Twinkles shot a sharp glance at Muffet, who was working at the table. But she was too self-contained to show her feelings.

"I suppose he will go," she said quietly.

"He will very likely go back to the Argentine. He has a ranch and some land out there."

"We seem to be losing all our friends," said Robin. "First Allister, and now its Gascoigne. I suppose Allister will come back with his mother for the funeral."

But Allister did not do so. Lady Eleanor returned without him. And a few days later Twinkles got the following letter from him:—

"DEAR LADY OF MY HEART,

I mean to obtrude myself once again upon you, for I will not be forgotten, and unfortunately I am unable to accompany my mother home. You will have heard of my brother's death. I won't say much about my feelings, now he is gone. I have wiped the past out with all its bitter memories, as I should like my own faults and misdeeds to be forgotten and forgiven. It is circumstances and not ill-will that keeps me absent.

But one day I shall suddenly appear in your toy kitchen, and set you dancing again before me in the firelight! I have lazed away, and made my mother laze, these winter months. And now what do you think I am going to do? I have been offered the post of Vice-Consul in Genoa under an old friend, and I start work to-morrow. That not being enough for my energy, I have undertaken to be a secretary of an Italian Emigration Society, and I shall be luring and shipping off Italians by the hundreds, to America. They say Vice-Consuls have all the work and none of the pay, so good-bye to my fiddle, and all that it means.

Do you remember my warning! The time will come when the extinct musician will claim compensation for all that has been taken from him. For that time he waits. A wreck of humanity may be washed up one day at the feet of the marble maid, who is responsible for the wreckage. Monotonous work always kills genius. But if this seems to you a matter for congratulation, send me yours. In any case I await reply.

Yours in dead earnest,

A Dying Musician."

"He's ridiculous," Twinkles muttered to herself. "But I will congratulate him that his idle days are over. I can do that. I'm thankful he is going to do something."

She did not show his letter to any one, but told Robin the contents of it.

"He's much better than he makes out," said Robin. "I wish he would come back."

Colonel Blair soon arrived at the Hall. He was a tall, delicate-looking man, a thorough Anglo-Indian, but he had a way of sauntering through the village and talking to all he met in his slow, pleasant voice, which made him very popular. Mrs. Blair took possession of him, drove him out, and seemed to have no intention of quitting the Hall. And then one day Kate, who knew all the news of the neighbourhood, came in and told Twinkles and Robin that there had been a dreadful scene between the young widow and her brother-in-law. She had spoken slightingly of Lady Eleanor, and Colonel Blair had looked her full in the face as he said:

"But my mother is returning here as mistress, as soon as you have settled where you want to live. You can have her house if you like. It is time we arranged matters."

"The footman told me Mrs. Blair raved and stamped like a lunatic, but out she has got to go! She thought the Colonel was soft and mild and easy to manage; but he knows how to put his foot down, and he's done it. And she's going up North to her own people this very next week, and Lady Eleanor is going back to the Hall."

Muffet was delighted when she heard this gossip. And then she came home entranced one morning, because Lady Eleanor had come out, and had had a little chat with her.

"She told me she was sorry to leave her peaceful little nest, but that she would never fail any son of hers. And she said Colonel Blair's health made her anxious, as she was afraid the English winters might not suit him, and he has been so many years in India. I wonder who will live in her house! There will be two empty houses now."

"Is Gascoigne going so soon?" asked Twinkles. "He has never been near us since his mother's death, which is rather strange, I think."

"He has been too busy. And the last fortnight he has been in town."

That very same day Muffet met him, as she was taking round her letters.

"I have come out on purpose to talk to you," he said.

"Then you must wait till my delivery is over," said Muffet, "for I cannot give my mind to anything while I am taking my letters round."

"Oh, these letters! How I hate them!" he said impatiently; but he walked beside her nearly the whole way, and then when she had left the last house, he began:

"I am giving up the Cottage almost directly."

"We feared you would. We shall miss you." Muffet's tone was a little unsteady.

"Will you? Do you remember making a certain promise to my mother? I want you to fulfil that promise now."

There was dead silence, then Muffet said, simply:—

"She asked me to comfort you when she was gone. I said I would, if you wanted me to. But what can I say or do? I don't think anyone can really comfort us when we lose our mothers. I have been through it as well as you, so I know."

"You *can* comfort me," said Gascoigne, huskily. "But perhaps you will feel you would rather not."

Another silence, then Gascoigne came to a standstill in front of her, and took both her hands in his.

"My mother hoped you would give yourself to me; can you, Muffet? I won't say as a lifelong comforter, for I think the man ought to be able to give more to the woman than she to him. It is from no selfish outlook—God knows—that I want you. I long to shield you from all the rough bits in life. It is because of this that I have hesitated in speaking to you. So before you give me your answer let me tell you more. I suppose I could support a wife, and live in idleness. I have enough for our needs, but I loathe an easy, luxurious idle life. One's whole being deteriorates. So I am determined to go out to the Argentine, and superintend my ranch there. And, later on, there is a small property in the North, that will be coming into my hands. It is let at present, but the lease is running out. A little time ago I should have said that I could ask no English girl to go out with me to the Argentine and rough it. But since I have known you and have seen how happy you all are living as you do, I am wondering if I mught venture to ask you to share my rough life for a few years?"

"Why do you want me?" said Muffet, trying to speak in a steady voice.

"Why? Oh, darling, because I have learnt to love you!"

And then Muffet heaved a little sigh.

"I hoped you would say that," she whispered. "You seemed so cold and calculating."

Gascoigne was not cold or calculating now, as he took her into his arms.

"I was nervous and frightened," he owned. "I was afraid you would say no. I was talking hard to give you time to think. Oh, Muffet, is it true? Can you, do you care for me a little bit?"

"A very big bit," said Muffet, trying to laugh, though tears were crowding into her eyes with the intensity of her emotions. "But I'm not an early Victorian girl, Gascoigne. I have too much muscle, and I don't want to be managed too much. Would you not be better pleased with a gentle, timid girl, who would never disagree with you, or have an opinion of her own?"

"I want no one but you."

"And you won't be too masterful with me?"

"I hope I shan't be. But I long to have a right to take care of you, and I'm coming to your door with you to-night, for I hate your being out after dark like this."

"I'm so glad you want me to share your life abroad," said Muffet a little later, "because there will be scope for my energies there, won't there? I can't tell you how I have missed all my golf and hockey and out-door sport. And I think this tramping round with letters has been my salvation. That is why I'm always gardening. I do love an outdoor life, and it is very close and small in our kitchen. I pant sometimes for more air and freedom. There! I'm talking about myself most selfishly, but you will understand."

Gascoigne would not come in. He left Muffet to tell her own tale, but he thrilled from head to foot when Muffet lifted her face to his of her own accord. And with his arm round her, he said:—

"We will help each other up, eh, darling? I feel so differently about good things since my mother was taken."

"We will learn together," responded Muffet. "I shan't rest till I have the same faith your mother had."

And with these words they parted.

When Muffet entered the kitchen, she found Twinkles and Poppet seated up at the table hat trimming. Poppet was leaving the next day, and she had been replenishing and mending her scanty wardrobe. She was just now expressing her dissatisfaction at the way Twinkles was placing a bow in her hat.

"It looks too old for me," objected Poppet, putting on the hat and standing before Robin. "Doesn't it make me look nearly fifty, Robin?"

"You ought to look old," said Twinkles; "for you're a governess."

"It doesn't look exactly smart," was Robin's verdict, as with head on one side he gazed at his sister.

"It looks dowdy!" said Poppet.

"You ought to look dowdy," said Twinkles.

"Because I'm a governess!" interrupted Poppet. "I know that's how you always end. But I don't mean to look dowdy or old. I'm a modern governess, not an old-fashioned one, and I like to look my best."

"Well, let me have another try," said Twinkles, good-humouredly. "I suppose even a bit of ribbon can be made to look rakish, if one tries. Here is Muffet. We'll ask her opinion."

"Muffet will say I've no business to waste my money in buying new ribbon," said Poppet.

"No," said Muffet. "I don't feel inclined to say anything to anybody to-night. The sooner you and Twinkles manage your money for yourselves, the better."

Twinkles looked up sharply. She saw that something had happened.

"Now launch your bolt," she cried. "You're going to tell us that you have secured a post for yourself as companion to your darling Lady Eleanor, or else that you've been promoted to be a post-mistress in some distant town!"

"Neither," said Muffet; but her rosy cheeks and shining eyes drew Robin's attention, and he guessed at once.

"You and Gascoigne are going to pair off," he said.

Muffet nodded.

"Not yet awhile. I feel rather selfish, as if I am being lifted out and away from our narrow life, and small means. But I won't be married for ages. I'll stay with you till better times come to us."

There was much excitement, and a good deal of talk. All were delighted at the news.

But Muffet got an opportunity of a quiet

word with Robin alone before she went to bed, and then she spoke with grave, soft voice.

"I'm not shirking my duty, as the eldest, am I, Cock Robin? I wouldn't leave you if I didn't know that Twinkles and you were happy together. And Gascoigne will be one of us now, won't he? And I think mother would have been pleased. Oh, how I wish she were here!"

Robin looked up earnestly.

"It's all first rate. Twinkles and I hoped it would happen. We shall miss you awfully, Muffet; but I know mother would have liked Gascoigne, and he knows how to take care of women."

"Yes," said Muffet, a little dubiously; "I suppose he does. I hope he knows, too, how to let women take care of him."

And then Robin laughed out merrily.

And Muffet went up to bed feeling that her world was carpeted with flowers and sunshine.

CHAPTER XIV.

A HARD TIME.

The next day, Gascoigne, of course, came round. Robin received him with such dignity that Twinkles beat a hasty retreat into the back kitchen to hide her amusement.

"We're very glad to hear the news," Robin began with outstretched hand, "for Muffet's happiness is our first thought, and I know you'll be good to her."

A twinkle came into Gascoigne's eye, but he replied gravely,

"I mean to be; she is one in a thousand."

Muffet laughed a little bashfully.

"Cut it short, Robin, and don't act the heavy father. This is an embarrassing moment for me. And do tell Gascoigne that my employment is going on as post-woman. Nothing is to be altered.

"The whole world is altered to me," said Gascoigne, gazing at her dreamily.

Then Twinkles reappeared and put them all at ease.

"I shall treat you as a brother at once," she said, "and ask you to lift in this basket of logs for me. You think men should always bear the burdens that come, don't you?"

"Yes," said Gascoigne, springing forward to obey, "most certainly physical burdens, for strength has been given to them for that purpose."

They were soon chatting merrily together, Gascoigne unfolding all his purposes and plans for the future, and if a shadow crossed his face and a softer intonation crept into his voice, they knew that he was thinking of his loss, and pitied him accordingly.

It was not very long before the whole village was acquainted with the engagement. Lady Eleanor and Miss Walpole both called to offer their congratulations, and Kate declared to the village gossips that it was a lucky man who got Miss Muffet for a wife, for she was a "young lady who could turn her hand to anything, and was ready for all emergencies."

In February, Gascoigne departed for the Argentine, with the understanding that Muffet would come out to him in a year's time. He was unhappy at leaving her, but nothing would induce her to marry him before that time.

"It is too much of a struggle at present to think of leaving Robin and Twinkles. I can make our money go much farther than they do. In a year's time Robin will be getting rent from his house, and we shall be eased all round."

"But darling, I have so much that I can spare—do let me."

"No, never! We are all proud! And we can manage perfectly!"

The "managing perfectly" was a hard task after Gascoigne left. Misfortunes came thick and fast. The weather was the worst they had experienced that winter. Twinkles had an accident with Robin's motor and the injuries to it were so severe that they could not afford to have it repaired, and it was laid aside. She escaped with a fractured ankle, which confined her to a couch, and Muffet's time was entirely occupied in household work, except when she went on her post rounds. She came home one night wet through from a driving storm of wind and rain, and the next morning could not get out of bed owing to violent rheumatic pains all over her body. Kate came in and sent for the doctor, who said it might be a case of rheumatic fever. This was fortunately averted, but a man from a distance was put on as postman, and the loss of the small weekly wage was much felt by the little household. Robin rose from his couch, and accomplished wonders on his crutches. Twinkles cooked and washed and mended from her couch, and Kate waited on the invalid upstairs.

They did not lose heart, but Robin's face was very sober one morning, when he handed

Twinkles a letter he had received. It was an offer to take a story of his on the old lines—an exciting, adventurous boy's tale.

"What am I to do, Twinkles? We are so very hard up. It isn't wicked to write those stories. It seems as if it is the only style that takes."

Twinkles was silent. She remembered Robin's emphatic words a short time ago. But then none of them were ill, and money was being earned. Now their expenses were greater and their means smaller.

"I can't advise you," she said. "It seems like a testing time, doesn't it?"

"If only I could hear news of that last venture of mine!"

"It has not come back to you yet, and that is a good sign. They have only had it about three months!"

Robin sighed as he turned the letter over in his hand.

"I want to write for God," he said in a low tone, "but it seems as if God doesn't want me to. And I don't know what I could write next."

Twinkles looked at him thoughtfully.

"We might wait a little longer. We are not actually starving."

"We shall be getting into debt this quarter."

"I'm afraid we shall. Well, as I say, I can't

advise you, Robin. But if this story is taken, I know what you could do next; you could take mother's story of the Heritages and make a book about each one. I know you would do it beautifully."

Robin's eyes kindled.

"Oh, I should *love* to do it. It would be continuing her work, and making her speak still to the world! I'll do it, Twinkles, and we'll make some publisher take my work. If we go up to London and beard them in their dens we'll do it! And I'll refuse this offer at once, I won't lower my standard!"

He sat down then and there with a bright face to refuse the chance of earning money.

"It's a testing time," he murmured. "I'll trust and not be afraid."

Poor Muffet tossed restlessly upon her bed upstairs. She felt that the house would go to pieces without her, and longed to be downstairs to see how things were going. Robin came to the foot of the steep little flight of stairs, and called out occasional encouraging words; but she would not be comforted and worried herself into a fever.

And then the last straw was, when influenza broke out virulently in the village, and Kate was prostrated with it. Mary was the only one left, and she was nursing Kate and minding the shop, with little time to spare to run in and help the invalids. They were hardly surprised when Robin sickened; for Kate had naturally kept up till the last and so passed on the infection. Twinkles was in despair and wired to Poppet to come home at once. The reply was prompt. "In bed with it myself; will come as soon as able."

Mrs. Handley was nursing her husband and boy, and did not know of their plight. Miss Walpole was nursing the General, who was in bed with the same complaint.

It was Lady Eleanor who eventually came to the rescue. Twinkles had managed to find a village girl to come in and help her; and she was hopping in and out of Robin's room with a bright face and anxious heart, when Lady Eleanor appeared.

"My dear child, what a chapter of horrors! I have missed our dear little post-woman so much. Let me see her first."

She went upstairs, and Muffet burst into tears when she saw her.

"I am a helpless log, and can't put my feet to the ground; everything is going wrong, and Robin will die, I feel he will. He is too good to live!"

Lady Eleanor smiled at her.

"Nonsense! I am going to take you all in hand. What would Gascoigne say if he knew of your plight? He would scold me well. I am very fond of Gascoigne, you know. I shall wire for a nurse from Mortonbury."

"Oh, please don't!" implored Muffet, who was too desperate to think of her words. "They eat so much and are such an expense."

"Then I shall take you away, and nurse you myself at the Hall."

A little thrill ran through Muffet at the vista presented to her. To be near Lady Eleanor for five minutes was bliss. What would it be to be in her house and in her care! But she was not a selfish girl, and put this enchanted vision from her.

"I think if you could take anyone, it should be Robin," she said. "But you mustn't do that, because influenza is so infectious, and I'm sure he is too bad to be moved, at any rate, at present."

"I will go down and see him, but I don't intend to leave you young people to yourselves any longer. Allister begged me to see more of you, and had it not been for my son's delicate health since he returned from India, I should have been here oftener."

Lady Eleanor's kind heart did reproach her, as she bent over and kissed Muffet's anxious puckered forehead.

"Smooth away your wrinkles," she said. "Better times are coming."

And then she went down and insisted upon

seeing Robin. He was almost light-headed, and kept murmuring to himself:

"It's only the testing time. I won't go back. Has the post come? Nothing yet? To-morrow —to-morrow."

"The doctor has been here," Twinkles said, "and can do nothing. We have just to keep him quiet, and give him plenty of nourishment."

"I should like to take him back to the Hall with me," said Lady Eleanor, "but I suppose he ought not to be moved at present. I wish his room was a little larger. How beautifully you keep your tiny house!"

Twinkles dimpled with pleasure.

"It isn't what it ought to be now, for we're a house of cripples. You can't think how helpless a bandaged foot makes you. I long to cut mine off; it is such a nuisance, but that would not remedy matters, would it?"

Twinkles laughed as she spoke; but her laugh had lost its merry ring; she was in reality nearer tears than laughter.

"It is good of you to think of having Robin," she went on; "later on, it would be lovely, that is if he gets well. You don't think he looks very ill, does he? You see, he is always a feverish subject, and suffers from his head."

"I am sure he ought to get well with good nursing, but you must have a nurse, child! I am going to send one in. Not a word now. The expense will be mine. You must all put your pride in your pockets till you are well again. How can you possibly attend to your sister upstairs, as well as your brother, when you have only one sound foot to stand upon?"

"Poor Muffet! She does get neglected. It is very lonely for her."

"Then let me take her right away from you till she is better, and then I am going to have Robin. I mean it. I will have her wrapped in blankets and brought to the Hall in a close carriage. I will ask Dr. Lemon if it will hurt her."

And the very next day Muffet's move to the Hall was accomplished, and she was established in a luxuriously furnished bed-room next to Lady Eleanor's.

She could hardly believe in her good fortune. It was a dream of delight to her. And one day she let Lady Eleanor have an inkling of her feelings.

"When I see you move about in my room it is joy," she said, "and when you sit down and put your hand upon my forehead I feel I could die happily."

Lady Eleanor laughed.

"You silly child! Why do you adore me so? I am not worth it. Don't make idols of human beings. I did when I was young, and broke my heart when I found my idol was made of very common clay.''

Muffet shook her head, but could not trust herself to speak. Her usual assurance and self-confidence forsook her, when she was talking to her beloved Lady Eleanor. She improved in health very rapidly, and if she showed anxiety at times about the Cottage, and its inmates, Lady Eleanor was always able to give her information that reassured her.

A nurse had been found, and sent to Robin. And he had turned the corner and was now doing well. Twinkles was able to give her foot the rest it required, and the little village girl worked well under her superintendence.

One afternoon, Twinkles was sitting in Robin's room, whilst the nurse was out walking.

''Isn't it strange,'' she said to him, ''how bad times come to an end? You think when you're in the middle of them that they will last for ever, but they pass, and you get through in a wonderful way! This day three weeks ago I was in abject despair.''

''Yes, God has helped us,'' said Robin, reverently. ''He sent Lady Eleanor at the right moment, not till then. If she had come before, we should have been too proud to take her help. It would have been of no use. But I am still worrying over our money affairs, and I expect Muffet is, too."

Twinkles got up from her seat.

"The letters have come," she said. "I am always expecting something good. I will run into the office and fetch them."

She left the room, and returned almost immediately, holding a letter aloft.

"Now, Robin, would you believe it? Your answer has come at last. The publisher's name is on the outside of the envelope. Now, prepare yourself for another bitter disappointment, or a lovely surprise. Are you ready for either?"

Robin took his letter with trembling fingers, and he read it with misty eyes. It was a letter that he treasured up for the rest of his life, for it was not only an acceptance of his story, but a warm-hearted appreciation of it, and an acknowledgment that it had quickened and stirred the heart of the reader as nothing else had for years.

"Send me others of the same sort," the publisher had written, "and you will be doing work for all eternity."

And then he mentioned terms which to Robin's inexperienced mind seemed incredibly generous. He and Twinkles were silent from the intensity of their emotions.

And then Robin said simply,

"I am glad I waited. Now I know that my work is wanted; I can go ahead!"

"It's glorious!" said Twinkles; and then she put her arms round him, and gave him a sisterly hug. "Oh, Robin, if I were you I would be the happiest creature on the face of the earth!"

"I expect I am!" he said with shining eyes. "After all, your legs and feet are not the best part of you."

"No, but since I have broken my ankle, I can feel for you as I have never felt before. It's awful to be crippled! But if I could write books, I would cheerfully sacrifice both my ankles. Oh, Robin, think of the bliss of helping thousands!"

"I think I shall dedicate my next book," he said slowly, "to mother, or in memory of her. For it will be her thoughts that I shall try to reproduce. And I shall set to work at once."

"Get a little stronger first. You haven't quite shaken off the flu!"

"I'm always a crock, but I can write."

He got his way; but when the doctor next called, and found him writing away, with an aching head, and high temperature, he turned to Twinkles sternly. He was an oldish man, and very brusque in manner.

"Why don't you chuck this pen and paper business in the fire? What's the good of me trying to bolster him up, if you help to knock him down again? Take the whole concern away, pens, ink and paper, every bit of it!"

"He worries more if he doesn't write, as it is such an effort to keep it in his brain," remonstrated Twinkles.

"Bosh! His brain ought to be lying fallow after an attack like this! If you can't manage him, I must find someone who can. How long has the nurse gone?"

"Four days. Please don't be cross. You don't understand what Robin's writing is to him!"

"I understand he is trying to kill himself, and you are helping him to do it!"

The doctor flung himself out of the house, and Twinkles looked aghast.

Robin began to laugh, in spite of his aching head.

"He is an old bear! I won't write any more to-day; I'm dreadfully tired!"

The next day Lady Eleanor called. Muffet was quite convalescent, and was wanting to come home.

"I am going to bring her back to-morrow, and take Robin instead. I am a very good nurse. The doctor has been talking to me of his iniquities!"

"He doesn't understand Robin as I do," said Twinkles, defending herself; "ever since he

HE IS TRYING TO KILL HIMSELF, AND YOU ARE HELPING HIM TO DO IT (Page 217)

was quite a little boy, he has always made up stories when he is lying ill, and it relieves him to write. Besides, he has had such encouragement, Lady Eleanor. Let me tell you."

Lady Eleanor listened with a smile to the good news.

"Yes," she said, "it must be a great temptation, but if he wants to get well quickly, he must exercise self restraint. And I will try and interest him in other ways, so that he may have a rest from his pen. Will you come to me, Robin, and try to keep from writing for a fortnight? You see, my dear boy, you don't want to prolong your illness. It is an anxiety and expense to your sisters. They would rather see you well, than earning money at the expense of your health."

"Yes, I am selfish," Robin acknowledged, lying back upon his pillows with a sigh, and giving up his manuscript paper to Twinkles. "I will try to make my mind a blank for a fortnight. It will be very good of you to have me. You are making your house into a hospital!"

So Muffet came home, and Robin went to the Hall, and Twinkles was perfectly miserable for the first few days without him. Yet his absence had the good result of bringing the two sisters nearer together than they had ever been before. Muffet's engagement had softened her;

she was more sympathetic; and tried to save Twinkles in many little ways, for her foot was not yet very strong.

"You ought to have a change next," Muffet said to her. "I can't tell you how good and kind Lady Eleanor is! I should like you to know her better, Twinkles. She is always thinking of making other people happy. I felt very selfish and wicked when I heard her talk, and saw the kind things she did! I think Colonel Blair is rather a trial to her. He is like Miss Walpole's brothers—selfish and exacting, and irritable. Lady Eleanor says it's his liver, and sometimes he is quite pleasant; but he had a bad attack when I first went there, and I was furious at the way he spoke to his mother. One day she came into my room and sat down with such a tired little sigh! 'What a blessing good health is,' she said; 'we are not half thankful enough for it; nothing in the world is a pleasure if we are ill.' 'I don't know about that,' I said, 'Robin is always ill more or less, but the least thing seems a pleasure to him—a fresh bunch of flowers or a new book or one of Twinkles' jokes,' and then she smiled so sadly I felt I longed to hug her. 'Yes,' she said, 'I was wrong to speak so; even sickness can be borne cheerfully.' "

"I think," said Twinkles, "that Robin may cheer the Colonel up. He is so fresh and eager about everything, that no one can mope in his company."

"Lady Eleanor's favourite son is Allister," pursued Muffet, looking at Twinkles thoughtfully; "she always brightens up when she gets a letter from him. She says he has become quite different lately, and has lost all his former indifference and laziness, but his letters are enough to make a cat laugh! She read me bits of them."

"What kind of bits?" Twinkles enquired, trying to speak indifferently, but in reality full of interest.

"Oh, he said he was working his legs and hands to death, but wasn't supposed to want a head; that was the *head* consul's affair. He only had to do what he was told, a thing he had never done since he was in the nursery, and his individuality was dead. But he said such a nice thing at the end of one of his letters. He was telling her how an Italian emigrant woman called down blessings on his head for what he had done for her. She said, 'May the good God bless you, and give you a crown of glory in the next world.' And he wrote, 'It set me thinking, and I'm now trying to develop the part of me, that told you when I was a youngster, and you had punished me for a breakage, that I was God's child as well as yours, and if *He* did not punish me *you* ought not?' I didn't know that

Allister ever thought about serious things, did you, Twinkles?"

"He never did, as far as I know, but it would be a good thing if he did develop his spiritual part; I hope he will."

And then Twinkles gave a little groan.

"What should I do if I had to live without Robin! Mrs. Handley thinks he won't live long. Wasn't that cruel of her to say such a thing to me! Robin helps us all with our spiritual parts, doesn't he? Oh, I could never, never live without him."

"I don't think he is the kind to die," said Muffet, consolingly, "though when I was ill I almost thought he might. He will never be strong, but there is nothing dangerous about his aches and pains; the doctors have said so."

"This old doctor says he is killing himself with his writing," said Twinkles, mournfully.

"That is only to frighten you into making him rest. He will get strong at the Hall. I felt quite different after three days. Lady Eleanor fed me up; and the luxury of it all was delicious!"

"It's a miserable life without Robin," said Twinkles, gazing at the empty couch disconsolately. "I shall never marry; I couldn't leave him."

"No, but he might live with you. I can't help wondering about the future sometimes.

And if—don't mind my saying it, Twinkles—if you only could like Allister, it would be a very happy thing for you and Robin. Because you know that eventually he will come to the Hall to live. Colonel Blair has not a long life before him—Lady Eleanor hinted as much. And I should like to think one day that she might be your mother-in-law."

"Don't!" said Twinkles, with hot, red cheeks. And then she ran out of the room forgetting her hurt foot.

Muffet looked after her and shook her head.

"I believe you are in love with him, for all your indifference!"

And Muffet was not very far from the truth.

CHAPTER XV.

ALLISTER'S RETURN.

Robin enjoyed himself thoroughly at the Hall. Lady Eleanor had a small room prepared for him as a bed-room which led out of the old library, so he had not to go up and down stairs. A comfortable couch was drawn up to the fire in the library, and there Robin used to spend his days. Very often he invaded the smoking room, which was the Colonel's particular sanctum. Sometimes the Colonel would saunter into the library, and seat himself with a shiver in the big easy chair by the fire, and talk to Robin in his slow, musical drawl, or listen, with a humorous twinkle in his eyes, to the boy's eager and enthusiastic views of life. The two struck up a strange friendship; and Lady Eleanor rejoiced to see it, as the Colonel was not sociable, and declared that visitors bored and fatigued him. He declined all invitations on the plea of ill health, and Robin soon discovered that it was Lady Eleanor who transacted all business for her son, and who interviewed daily the head bailiff, and discussed all necessary estate affairs with him.

One rainy afternoon the Colonel came into the library, asking Robin if he knew where Lady Eleanor was.

"She has gone to Montonbury in the brougham," was the prompt reply. "It is some committee meeting, I believe, about the board schools."

"Confound the board schools! Here's a wire that she ought to answer."

He threw himself into the chair as he spoke.

"Couldn't you answer it for her?" Robin queried.

"No," he replied, "I'll let it slide. It's only about some roofing for one of the farms. What atrocious weather! It's cold enough for snow."

"We don't feel the weather in here," said Robin, closing his book with a bang. "And I've been in such a jolly hot place all this afternoon, that I should be glad to be cold for a change."

"Eh?"

"I've been reading a stunning travel book I fished down from the bookcase, all about the desert and the excavations round Babylon. I felt I was there. Don't you do that sometimes? The sky was a hard, bright, hot blue, the heat simmered up from the yellow sand, and there was hardly any shade under the dried-up palm trees. I simply gasped, and longed for a drink, and then just as some Arab merchants were coming along—you came in!"

"Sorry to have broken the spell! What a baby you are!"

Robin gave his funny little chuckle.

"I get much more fun out of books than you do."

"I'm sure you do. There's not much sport I get, now-a-days."

"You see," said Robin, putting his arms behind his head and pillowing it upon them, whilst he looked at the Colonel with his bright eyes, "I've always had to live in books. I never can have the real thing, you know!"

"Poor little beggar!" said the Colonel. "It's hard luck on you. I've had my day, I suppose. You never will! Well, I don't know that in the long run it's any advantage!"

"But we don't always reckon with the long run," said Robin.

The Colonel smiled.

"We don't indeed, young Plato."

"Don't call me that, it sound so priggish. And I have a jolly good time in books. I have been in all quarters of the world. If I had a library like this I'd feed on it till I burst!"

It was an inelegant term, but Robin spoke hotly. He added—

"And if I can't do things like most fellows, I

have a jolly good time imagining I can. And everyone can't have the same heritage."

"What is yours?" asked the Colonel.

"Suffering," said Robin, earnestly. "When I was a tiny chap my mother explained it to me by a little allegory which has burnt itself into my soul. Would you like to hear it?"

The Colonel nodded, and in a low, sweet voice the boy told the story of the different heritages to which people are called.

The man of the world listened with amusement and interest, but he was more touched than he cared to show.

"So you think your life work is to suffer, do you?" he asked.

"To suffer—and be strong!" said Robin with emphasis.

"What has mine been, I wonder?" said the Colonel, a twinkle coming into his sleepy eyes.

"I should say you were meant to be a knight or a ruler."

Colonel Blair shook his head.

"Then I have never fulfilled my Creator's intentions. My rôle now is to suffer for the rest of my days, and I know they will not be very long. Can you give me your recipe for making suffering bearable?"

Robin's face lit up in an instant.

"When I'm pretty bad, I say to myself, 'I delight to do Thy will, O God,' for if it's God's will that I should suffer, of course I ought to like to do it. Nobody—the greatest saint or warrior or ruler on earth can do *more* than God's will. So it makes us quits, doesn't it. Doing our King's will is the highest ideal for the most gifted, the most strong; and it's so splendid to think that the weakest and poorest on earth are shoulder to shoulder with the greatest and noblest in this! I sometimes think when I'm stirred up by reading of a splendid charge in a tight corner on a battlefield, 'they dash on to meet suffering and death with enthusiasm and joy. Can't I lie still and meet my pain in the same spirit?' Because I needn't tell you that I'm awfully cross and impatient sometimes."

There was a little silence. Then Robin added softly: "And when one thinks of our King's Son coming into our world on purpose to go through suffering for us, and saying just before His agony was coming on 'the Cup which my Father hath given Me, shall I not drink it?' it makes one feel rather ashamed of not drinking our small cup, doesn't it?"

"You're above and beyond me now!" said the Colonel, but he was silent for some minutes, and then began to chat on other matters.

After this, Robin had many an earnest talk with him. He spoke naturally of the things he loved and reverenced, and had no self-consciousness or awkwardness in doing so. The Colonel listened and did not ridicule him. He was getting a new glimpse of life as it might have been for him, and of what it might be still; and though at first amusement and curiosity preponderated, he soon began to ponder, and weigh matters as he had never done before.

Lady Eleanor grew very fond of Robin. She took him for drives, which were a keen delight to him. She brought her work into the library, and talked to him of his mother and of his old home, and of his sisters. Muffet seemed most in her thoughts. She was strangely silent about Twinkles, but Robin was not; he was full of her praises, and of all she did, and bore, and of her irrepressible gaiety.

His health and spirits improved day by day, and though true to his promise never to touch pen or paper, he was surprised to find how little he desired to do it. His mind was feeding and taking in instead of giving out, and it was an excellent change of life for him. When the time came for him to leave, both the Colonel and his mother were genuinely sorry to part with him. The Colonel told him he would look in sometimes, and bring his pipe with him to have a chat, and Robin's delighted acquiescence gratified the Anglo-Indian, who was astonished to find what a warm place the cripple boy occupied in his heart.

It was a gala day when Robin returned to the Cottage. Twinkles had been up since daybreak, cleaning and polishing, and having everything shining with much elbow grease and any amount of energy. Muffet and she had prepared an extra good tea, and they received Robin as if he had been away for a twelvemonth, instead of three weeks. The little kitchen was looking its very best, and Robin got upon his couch with a happy sigh.

"It's home to me," he said. "And now, Twinkles, make me laugh! We have had no fun at the Hall."

Twinkles had no difficulty in complying with his request; she was in her maddest, gayest spirits, and executed a *pas seul* with the broomstick round the kitchen.

"I'll never let you go again, Cock Robin!" she declared. "We poor hens have wailed in the dust for you! Muffet's house-keeping purse has been the gainer, for we have had no appetites, and I haven't made a single cake whilst you have been away!"

In a very short time they had all settled down again to their usual routine, and as the spring came on, Twinkles was busy making extensive arrangements for her cyclists' lunches and teas. Robin assured her that there was no need to work so hard, for he would be earning regularly, he hoped, now, by his pen. His poems were appearing in print, and he had already received the first proofs of his book.

It was a great excitement and interest to them all, for though his stories had been accepted, and were running in boys' magazines, this was his first book. Twinkles and he pored over the proofs with much anxiety. It was a laborious task correcting them, but it was a labour of love, and they longed to see the book in the glory of its first binding.

Easter came round again, and Poppet appeared. She had had a trying term, for one after the other in the Vicarage had been ill with influenza, and she herself had had it very badly.

Nothing but sheer necessity would have kept her away, she declared, when she knew she might have helped them in their stress at the Cottage. She was taller and thinner, and was growing quite a pretty girl. They had a lot to talk about.

"Poppet," said Muffet suddenly, "what would you do if we all went away and married?"

"Married and went away," corrected Robin, "but you must leave me out of that possibility."

"Oh, well, you would be with Twinkles if she married. We all know that."

"I am not going to marry," Twinkles asserted.

"I shouldn't mind at all," said Poppet quite cheerfully. "I am perfectly happy where I am. I shall stay with Mrs. Gates as long as she wants me—I love her, and she likes me—and perhaps one day I shall marry a very nice curate who will become a bishop!"

"Every girl doesn't marry," said Twinkles rather sternly. "There is need for single women in the world for all the work that others leave undone."

"Of course," said Poppet. "I only meant that you needn't try to arrange for me to be the old maid of the family, because I am a governess."

"You shan't be a governess in a few years' time when I go back to my house again," said Robin. "I shall have to write a good many books; but my head is simply bursting with ideas, and I think I shall write faster than the publishers will take them. It is so jolly to be earning money!"

"But that's what I feel," said Poppet. "I shan't want to stop earning, any more than you do. It gives me such an important feeling to know that I am supporting myself."

"I think it is splendid of you, Poppet," said Muffet warmly. "You have done it so quickly and quietly. I almost envy you."

"Well," said Twinkles, "our year of effort is coming to an end. Things will be easier now.

When did Mr. Mackenzie say he was going to forward us some rent, Muffet?"

"Next June."

"We shall be able to take a bigger house perhaps."

"Oh, no," remonstrated the cautious Muffet; "we are quite comfortable here; I am sure the rent will only ease us all round in our present circumstances. Perhaps we can get a young servant; then you would not have to work so hard, Twinkles. We could give up the Cyclists' teas. I hate them."

"I rather enjoy them," said Twinkles. "And I have learnt such a lot about cooking and house-work, that this year's struggle has done me good and not harm."

"I expect it has done us all good," said Muffet thoughtfully, "but it has been very hard sometimes."

"It has been our testing time," said Robin brightly. "I've nearly gone under several times, but the worst has passed now—and we'll never doubt again, for God means to bring us through. It's quite easy to Him if we trust Him."

A little silence fell on the young people, which was broken by a peremptory tap at the door. Twinkles' face paled and flushed at once, for she knew the tap. The next moment Allister Blair walked into the kitchen.

"Thought I'd look you up," he said in his brusque fashion. "But this time I've been to the mother first. Well, how are things going?"

There was a delighted welcome from all, except Twinkles, and it was she to whom Allister turned first of all.

"You look at me as if I am a ghost," he said, smiling at her with rather a wistful look in his eyes. "I told you I would come back, didn't I?"

"Have you given up your billet?" she asked gravely.

"No," he replied. "I'm having a few days' holiday. I don't mean to give it up, though my brother has been wanting me to come home, dismiss our bailiff, and be agent myself for our property. He says he can't see to things, and it is too much for the mother."

"Oh, you ought to do it!" cried Muffet. "Dear Lady Eleanor ought to be spared all worries in her old age."

He shook his head, but his eyes never left Twinkles' face.

"I am a money grubber. I have given up my fiddle, and lost all my musical atmosphere. I am going through with my job, but"—here he addressed Twinkles with grave emphasis—"I told you I would return to claim compensation!"

Muffet drew Poppet quietly out of the room. Robin fidgetted on his couch uneasily. He saw something in Allister's eye that meant business, and getting up from his couch he said to Twinkles,

"I'm going into my room for a spell. I must finish some writing there. There's a fire, so don't fuss——"

"Don't leave me," pleaded Twinkles, but Robin was gone. Allister laughed, and his happy, ringing laugh made Twinkles smile.

"You are afraid of me!" he said.

"Not a bit! You have come back much too soon."

"Do you think so? I've been sent on business to London. Been there two days—and done it in first rate style—and now I have four days holiday before I return. Only four, but I can tell you, I mean them to be four golden days of compensation!"

Twinkles said nothing. She was standing on the hearthrug by the fire, and did not move.

Allister drew a chair forward.

"Do sit down," he said. "A man can always talk better when he is above a woman's level."

"You are too ridiculous!" said Twinkles. "Nothing would keep you from talking."

But she sat down, and Allister stood in her

place, upon the hearthrug, with his back to the fire. His eyes wandered round the room, and came back to her face.

"I have dreamed of this moment ever since I left you," he said very quietly. "What a heavenly little kitchen this is! What could one want more? You and I in a little home like this, and Robin close at hand, but in the other room when necessary!"

Then Twinkles looked up very determinedly.

"Now, Mr. Blair, I hope you have not come here to talk nonsense. I am very, very glad you are working, and I am sure your mother must want to see as much of you as possible, so you must not stay here long——"

He interrupted her.

"I have told you that I came back to claim compensation. You have spoiled a musician's life. You have turned him into a matter-of-fact, common official drudge. Now, what are you going to give him? Don't answer quickly. I want you to look me straight in the face for a moment. I'm in desperate dead earnest, Twinkles. You have altered my whole life, my aims, my ideals. You have turned me topsy turvy, and inside out! You have shaken my spirit and soul to pieces—and it's not a bit of use your disclaiming all responsibility, for you have begun to meddle with my individuality, and mould me, and—and possess me, and you'll just have to go on doing it all your life, only in a closer, dearer way."

He was leaning down to her now and had got hold of her hands. He was, as he said, in desperate earnest. Twinkles felt his dominant power over her. She tried to meet his gaze; but her eyes fell beneath his passionate pleading.

"I told you long ago," she said, "I want a man to help me to rise."

"And I want a woman to help me," he retorted, "and by God's help we'll do it together. You have begun to make a man of me, my darling, and you must go on. I've thrown off my sloth, and indifference to our Faith, and I'm learning daily that there is another life besides this present one. There's an awfully good sort of chaplain out in Genoa—he and I are great pals—shouldn't have looked at him a year ago—but I seize everything that comes by to enable me to climb—and it's all for you—and for your sake."

"Then it ought not to be," said Twinkles. "No one ought to try to be religious to please any human creature—only God. He made us; and He owns us; He has the right to our first affections!"

"Yes, child, yes—I know that, but you have started me on the right track, and having done this, don't you see how responsible you are!"

"Oh," said Twinkles with a little sigh, "I don't know what to do! You are so vehement! Let me ask you this: If I said I would have nothing to do with you, would you go back from all that you are aiming at now?"

It was a test. Allister drew a hard breath, and then all his extravagance in speech melted away. He replied slowly and simply—

"To be quite honest, I don't think I should. The taste of the new life is better than the old."

Twinkles' scruples fled. She raised her face with glowing eyes to his.

"Then I will be yours, Allister. My heart has been yours ever since you left. I am not really good, but we will help each other, as you say, and if I can't lean upon you at first, it will make me lean harder upon God—and I do admire you awfully for setting to work as you have done. And—and—oh, please have mercy—and don't smother me!"

Half an hour after, Robin and the others were summoned back. Allister could not conceal the triumph in his heart.

"She has given me compensation," he said, "and you must congratulate me. Now, what can we do to celebrate this occasion?"

"If you had your violin we could have a dance," said Muffet, laughing. "That was how you first came into our lives. I remember how aghast I was to see Twinkles and Bumbles careering all over the kitchen."

"My poor fiddle! I have brought it over, but have locked it up tight until I knew my fate. Well, aren't you going to offer me your congratulations?"

They gave them to him most heartily, Robin the most warmly of them all. And then Muffet disappeared into the back kitchen. She came back with a coffee pot in her hands.

"We have no wine to drink your healths," she said, "but we'll drink it in coffee. Only Twinkles will have to make it. Her coffee is always excellent."

"She's good all round," said Robin; "I hope you don't mean to take her away just yet?"

"I shall never leave you," Twinkles said, quickly.

"Look here," said Allister, with twinkling eyes, "this is *my* night, and you are—if you are a well regulated and properly brought up girl—to be wholly and entirely engrossed with the thoughts of me. No one else comes into the ring with us. The world around us retires into a dim, foggy distance. I see only you, I live, I breathe only for you, and you see only me. Robin is an awful good sort, he can stand close to us and admire us, but we shall not feel his presence."

Twinkles laughed out merrily.

"I never shall be sentimental; you'll be terribly disappointed."

But when he rose to go, Twinkles followed him to the open door, and they stood there together for a few minutes looking up into a star spangled heaven.

"What will your mother say?" Twinkles whispered. "I'm no match for you. A portionless girl, and not even beautiful."

"My mother wished me success before I came. She will come to see you to-morrow."

"Oh, Allister, we will walk heavenwards—promise me again that you will help me. I do feel that God is very good in giving me your love."

Allister looked down upon her with grave eyes.

"If you feel that my poor love comes to you through such a channel, may Heaven help it to be worthy of such. And I consider here, under God's dominion of stars, that we are brought together and bound together in His sight for ever. Soul to soul—death will not part us!"

"Amen!" whispered Twinkles solemnly.

It was a solemn wooing for such gay young spirits. But Allister was compounded of many parts, and his deeper nature was not always drawn to the surface. To-night his depths had been reached, and Twinkles knew it. She parted with him, with joy welling up into her heart.

The next day Lady Eleanor appeared. It was rather an ordeal for Twinkles, but she was her simple natural self, and responded very sweetly to Lady Eleanor's affectionate greeting.

"I did not know whether my boy would meet with success or not, but he returned to me last night a new creature. Oh! Twinkles, my dear child, you have it in your power to make or mar him! So few girls are conscious of their tremendous influence over a man's character. And Allister is emotional and impressionable. He has the artistic temperament which needs patience and tact to cope with it. I would not hide his faults from you. He is not perfect, but he has a heart of gold if it can only be reached. People think him shallow and superficial; he delights with the contrariety of his nature to make them think so. But I, his mother, know him better; and you will know him and love him as I do. I have been thankful that his music has been more to him than the society of women. Now I am willing that his music should retire to the background, if he has gained and can keep the love of a good, sensible girl."

"But I tell Allister that I do not consider myself a rival to his music," said Twinkles, smiling; "I love it as much, or nearly as much as he does."

Lady Eleanor leant forward and kissed her. "You will be a dear little daughter to me," she said.

Muffet, standing by, turned away suddenly to hide the tears in her eyes. Her romantic love for Lady Eleanor had never been quenched.

"Oh, if I could be her daughter!" was the thought of her heart.

Lady Eleanor was a woman of perception. She put out her hand and laid it gently on Muffet's arm.

"This will give me the right to act as a second mother to you all," she said. "And since my grand-children have left me, I have felt a lonely old woman. You must let me see a great deal of you all. I shall expect to do so. It will be my right."

"Oh," said Muffet, with a little choke in her throat, "it will be heavenly to have you to advise us about things! We have stumbled along as best we could, but I have longed to be able to talk to someone sometimes, who could give us counsel."

Lady Eleanor smilingly promised to befriend them as much as she could; and when she left, Twinkles declared that she would never be shy or frightened of her again.

Her visit had been a complete success.

CHAPTER XVI.

A HOLIDAY.

"But we don't want to break up our dear Cottage." It was Twinkles who spoke.

She was standing by a blazing fire in the big drawing room of the Hall, looking very pretty in her simple black evening dress with a cluster of white roses at her breast. Her mischievous eyes were dancing with fun as she gazed up into Allister's face. It was nearly dinner time; but Lady Eleanor was not yet downstairs, and the young people had the room to themselves. It was Twinkles' first dinner at the Hall. Muffet had been asked to accompany her, but had declined. Poor Muffet did not possess an evening dress, and Twinkles' gown had been obtained and made with some difficulty. She, and the little village dressmaker, had taken only two days to make it; but it had been hard work, and Twinkles was conscious of its defects. Allister told her that she and her dress were perfect; but Twinkles shook her head at this lovelike speech.

Now she was being importuned by him for a speedy marriage.

"Come back to Italy with me. We will have three weeks mooning, and then Robin shall join us."

"How do you think he could take that long journey by himself?"

"Then we'll take him with us."

"But we don't want to break up our dear cottage."

Allister looked at her in silence.

And then Twinkles put a hand on each of his broad shoulders, and gave him a light, fairy-like kiss.

"I won't be coerced by looks! Tell me, you unpractical musician, have you a house for me? Servants?"

Allister's look was a blank one now.

"Houses! Servants! We are not such hum-drum creatures as to need them. We'll feast on dew and honey, and wander through the olive woods."

"And what about your work? I will *not* marry an idler, I told you so long ago."

"But isn't it usual for bride and bridegroom to have a honeymoon?"

"Yes, certainly—but afterwards. Oh, Allister, do be sensible. Go back to Genoa; work away, and write some of your delicious letters to me. I will work too, and then, perhaps, next autumn."

"And waste the lovely hours of summer?

I don't believe you want to come into my life.''

Twinkles' reproachful gaze made him apologetic at once; and then Colonel Blair came into the room.

''What am I to call you?'' he asked the young girl. ''Have you no other name but Twinkles?''

''It's the dearest little name that was ever given to anyone,'' said Allister, dreamily. ''It sets one thinking of stars lovingly winking and blinking down on us poor puny atoms of humanity. Only one star for me—''

''Oh, Allister, do talk sense!'' interrupted Twinkles briskly. ''My real baptismal name is Pauline, Colonel Blair, but it sounds too grand and good for me.''

Twinkles was in reality rather shy of her future brother-in-law, but his warm liking for Robin drew her towards him.

When Lady Eleanor came into the room a few minutes later, she found Twinkles chatting away to the Colonel with perfect composure. She had welcomed Twinkles very warmly, and if she had wished her favourite son to have made a more successful match from a worldly point of view, she did not show it by word or look. In fact, she was grateful to the girl for rousing her boy from his easy going self-indulgent life.

The dinner was only a family one, and after it was over, Lady Eleanor took Twinkles into her confidence. She placed her in a comfortable chair by the fire and said:—

"Now, till Allister comes in to monopolise you, I want to tell you about him. You are a sensible girl and a good one. You know his failings as well as I do; he is unpractical and dreamy and has only lately roused himself to take an interest in other people. His brother is, I am afraid, even now trying to persuade him to settle down here. You know that my son George is not at all strong. The doctor thinks very seriously of his case—and I feel that sooner or later Allister will be master here. But much as I would like to have him home, I do not want him to settle down into a life of ease at present. And, knowing the past, I fear that as his brother's agent, Allister would not be a success. He has not been trained in orderly, methodical and business-like ways. His present work out in Italy is doing him a lot of good. I want him to keep to it, and I want you to influence him to do so."

"But that is what I am trying to do," said Twinkles eagerly, "only I am sure he ought to do it alone. I don't think he wishes to give it up—I am sure he does not."

"He wants you to marry him at once and go out with him. I suppose you cannot do it?"

Twinkles noted the wistfulness in the mother's voice.

"You don't trust Allister as much as I do," she said, half laughing. "You want me to accompany him everywhere to keep him straight and make him work; but I'm sure I should be making a mistake if I did that. I have told him that I could marry no man who wants to be bolstered up by a woman. And dear Lady Eleanor, he has a power stronger than I helping him now. I don't believe he will fail. I do think his work as vice-consul out there is doing him good. As you say, he has learnt to take others into his life, and the more he does for them, the better it will be for himself."

Lady Eleanor smiled at Twinkles' glowing eyes.

She did not feel vexed at the young girl's assurance about her lover. She only realised, as many a mother has to do, that the love of a promised wife has more effect on a man's character than the love of his mother, however great and true that love may be.

"Well, dear, you and he must settle it between you, but I wanted to say this, that if you do go out to him, I should like to have Robin with me. George is so fond of him, that it would be a real pleasure to him. And he could stay with me just as long as he liked."

"It is awfully good and kind of you," said

Twinkles, thoughtfully, "but Muffet is not going to marry yet. And somehow or other, neither of us can bear to be the first one to break up our little home. We have been so happy in our Cottage, and we shall never be the same again when once we scatter."

"No, you will not," said Lady Eleanor with a little sigh.

And then they sat silent till Colonel Blair and Allister joined them.

"Put a wrap on and come round the garden with me," said Allister, coming up to Twinkles; "if we were in Italy the trees would be covered with blossoms and the gardens a dream of beauty. Our English springs ought to be discarded. They're frauds and pretend to be what they're not!"

Twinkles got a shawl and threw it round her. Allister led her down an old rose walk through pergolas that were just beginning to be covered with fresh green, and brought her to an old sun dial.

"Now," he said, drawing her into his arms, "isn't this a fitting place to talk of our love? Our early Victorian drawing-room gives me the blues!"

"Oh, you emotional creature!" laughed Twinkles, as she rested her head on his shoulder and looked up at him with her sunny eyes; "is your love such a poor thing that it can be quenched by its surroundings? Could you not love me if we were in a top London attic with bare boards and an empty cupboard?"

"Couldn't I?" returned Allister fervently; "I feel I could be in bliss in a coal cellar if you were with me. What has the mother been saying to you?"

"She is anxious for you to return to Italy."

"George is not keen upon it."

"So your mother said. What do you feel about it yourself?"

"I want you to come with me, and so does the mother."

"Do you know why?"

"Why my mother wants it?"

He laughed and added:—

"She knows me better than you do, my darling. She thinks I shall never do much good alone."

"Oh, Allister, aren't you ashamed to put it into words? Wouldn't you be ashamed to take a wife in order that she should make you work?"

"I don't think you would." said Allister, looking at her meditatively. "My will has never left me. Besides, if I choose I can just set you dancing. My fiddle is my master and will become yours."

"No, never. I would break its strings if it made you lazy!"

"Ah, don't talk of it! It's like talking of twisting babies' limbs. My poor fiddle! You have wrenched it out of my life for the time, but oh, dearest sweetheart, you're worth it!"

And then Allister refused to talk sense, and Twinkles gave herself up to the witchery of the hour, and to her lover's whispered words.

But she would not stay long in the garden.

"It is not kind to your mother. I am her guest."

They retraced their steps to the house, and again Allister pleaded that she should return to Italy with him; but Twinkles remained firm.

"Next autumn, come back and fetch me."

And eventually Allister resigned himself to do so.

When Twinkles got home that evening, she found Robin had had one of his bad attacks and Muffet came out of his room with an anxious face.

"I wish you would go in to him, Twinkles. His head seems so bad and he is very feverish."

In a second Twinkles was bending over her brother.

"I ought not to have left you," she said.

Robin looked up at her, trying hard to smile; but his eyes were heavy and his brow contorted with pain.

"Have you settled the day?"

"What day?"

"Your wedding day."

"Now, Robin, have you been worrying over me? I believe you have. I am not going to marry for ages. I have told Allister so."

"He—he said you must go back with him."

"And I have told him I will not."

Then Twinkles laid her curly head on the pillow close to Robin's.

"Oh, Cock Robin, I don't think I shall marry after all. I would much rather live with you. I wish—I almost wish Allister had never come into our life. He is so insistent and he will never, *never* be to me what you are. You are my mainstay, my pilot, my rock. You never change!"

Tears were in Twinkles' eyes. Robin smiled, as he tried to raise himself from his pillows.

"You're a goose, Twinkles! I'm making out a lovely future. You will be a lady of the Manor here, and I shall live—perhaps if Lady Eleanor will let me—in the Dower house. She told me the other day that she is tired of it, and if she ever left the Hall again she would go abroad. I shall be a rich man then, and you will come running to me when you are tired or cross, or want advice. And I have been talking over things with Muffet, and I don't think I shall ever go back to my house again. We have made so many friends here, haven't we? And that house of mine will be one of my sweet memories to think about in my pain. It is mixed up with mother; I like to think it slipped away from me when she did. We have lovely things in life, Twinkles, but they will not last for ever. And sometimes the memory of them is sweeter than the experience."

"You are talking too much," remonstrated Twinkles.

But Robin went on:—

"I want you to see that we have happiness in front of us. And if I could get a glimpse of Italy—not just when you go to Allister but afterwards—Lady Eleanor has said I can go with her and meet you out there—why, Twinkles don't you see what joy you will bring to me by marrying Allister?"

"I sometimes think that you are an arrant humbug," said Twinkles; "but I shan't let you say another word! Good night. God bless you."

Robin lay very still after she had left him, and then he murmured to himself,

"She says I get absorbed in my books, so it is only fair that she should have an object to absorb her. We shall never be apart in spirit. No—I am glad for her, and only a tiny bit sorry for myself. And I won't be such a beast as to wish to keep her tied to a helpless cripple all her life!"

His head still ached, but peace reigned in his heart, and sleep soon came to him, and comforted and refreshed his weary body.

Meanwhile Twinkles was called into Poppet's bed-room.

"Twinkles, are you tired? I want to have a talk with you. I am sure you and Allister will be married soon. He won't wait, and I don't wonder. Don't laugh at me, for I want to help you."

Poppet looked very sweet and serious, but a regular child in her blue dressing-gown, with her hair over her shoulders. She was in the act of brushing it, and now rapidly plaited it up in a thick tail as she talked. Twinkles sat down on the edge of the bed and waited. She and Poppet were beginning to understand each other better now, and rarely squabbled as they used to do.

"I know how you'll feel about Robin," Poppet went on; "but that is what is worrying him. He is afraid you are going to sacrifice yourself for him, and he'll fret his heart out if you do. I want you to feel that you can count upon me to come home and take up the housekeeping when you go. I think it would be too much for Muffet to do alone. She does so much in the garden and out of doors that she couldn't get through everything without help. And then, if Robin and I fitted in together, when Muffet marries, we could still be together. I would do my very best to look after him and cheer him up. I really have learnt a lot since I have been with Mrs. Gates.''

''It's very good of you,'' said Twinkles, ''for I know how you love being where you are, but I assure you, Poppet, that I shall never be long parted from Robin. He and I will still live our lives together whether I'm married or unmarried. Allister knows this. And I don't intend to be married till next autumn. Wild horses won't drag me. No, Robin must come to Italy if I go out there. That will be a real joy to him. Now, don't make any more plans, there's a dear. I'm very tired and I want to go to bed.''

The sisters parted for the night, but when Twinkles got into her room she said to herself, with a smile and sigh:—

''And all this is just because I have been out to dinner!''

The next morning Allister arrived immediately after breakfast in Colonel Blair's motor.

Robin was better, but lay in the little kitchen looking white and weary. Twinkles was just beginning to make a steak pudding for dinner. She wrung her hands in dismay when Allister entered the room.

''You must give us time to get through our morning duties,'' she said, trying to speak sternly, but smiling in spite of herself, as Allister presented her with a bunch of lilies of the valley and embraced her with fervour.

"We are all as busy as can be! Muffet is sowing seeds in the garden, and Poppet is washing up the breakfast things and Robin is going to read me his last chapter. We have no time to frivol."

"But that is exactly what you are going to do, every one of you," cried Allister gaily. "I have got extension of leave—a whole fortnight, and I am going to metamorphose you from bees into butterflies. Have you troubled to look out of doors this morning? Have you not heard Spring's insistent voice calling you out? We'll make a bonfire of Muffet's seeds and Poppet's dishes, and your pudding, and Robin's chapter. And we'll cast duties behind our backs and have a thoroughly dissipated day."

Twinkles shook her head at him, but Robin's eyes gleamed. He hurriedly folded his MS. papers together.

"We will, Allister," he cried. "I've heard the birds singing this morning and I pant for the open. We'll cast dull care behind our backs. What is your plan?"

"I have the motor for the day and the chauffeur. The five of us can pack in comfortably. Drop everything, and be ready in five minutes and lock up the house. We won't take any notice of time. I love to ignore him."

"You need not tell us that," said Twinkles, laughing. "I believe the air will do Robin a world of good, so we'll do it. That is, if I can persuade Muffet to leave her beloved garden."

"I'll manage her," said Allister, disappearing through the back kitchen.

He, as usual, got his way. In a very short time Robin was comfortably settled with cushions in the motor, and the Cottage was left empty. "You have an ill-regulated mind," Twinkles told Allister, "but for once in a way we'll give in to you!"

And then they started, and as Allister said, spring, in all its loveliness was around them. The air was fresh, but not too cold, the roads free from dust, and the fresh sweet green in the hedges, and upon the trees, was a continual delight to their eyes.

Robin lay back in a perfect trance of happiness and Twinkles looking at him felt her heart leap within her at the thought of the pleasure she might in the future bring into his life.

She laid her hand gently on Allister's arm.

"You are a dear!" she said. "I think you love to give happiness."

"Sunshine and air, are free gifts, but they're not used half enough," he replied; then he added, as he looked at her: "This is only a foretaste of what we shall do by and bye, but

I'm going to enjoy my paradise to-day without any memories or anticipations."

"Where are we going?" asked Muffet.

"To the top of Exmoor—Dunkery beacon, if you like, but no—I will take you to a pet corner of mine—a little haven of beauty."

"We have brought no food with us—you hurried us so."

"There's a luncheon basket with us, bursting with provisions."

"Did you prepare all this beforehand?"

"I thought of it while I was shaving," said Allister gravely. They all laughed, and he joined them.

"Don't you know our motto?" he continued. "'*To think is to do.*' I'm never long in carrying out my plans."

"I don't like that motto," observed Muffet gravely; "that is the way murders are carried out. We oughtn't to trust our impulses."

"You mustn't preach to-day," Twinkles said. "Let us be gay—Allister's impulses are generally good."

So they careered along through sweet Somerset lanes, dipping into valleys and coombes, and mounting up gradually to the bracing air of the moors. And then at last Allister called a halt. The car had brought them to bracken covered slope, with a tumbling brook of clear grey water.

"We have a climb before us, but we'll rig up a hammock for Robin, and he won't have to walk a step."

Robin at first objected to this, but Allister insisted; he and the chauffeur slung him into a thick plaid, and the two strode along, carrying him with perfect ease to the summit. There was a grove of old beeches on one side of the slope. Under a group of these at the top they put him down, and told him to look around him. It was a lovely scene, for the sea lay stretched out below them, and the moor ran down in wooded slopes to the cliffs. And as Robin gazed he saw a group of wild deer in the distance. They had been browsing but seemed to scent the approach of human beings, for their heads were raised with keen alertness, and in a minute they had trotted down the slope and were lost to sight in the undergrowth of the coombe. The girls were loud in their admiration of the moor. Luncheon was unpacked and was a triumph of sudden preparation.

"Our old cook is accustomed to send out lunches for shooting parties. Half an hour's notice is sufficient for her," said Allister unconcernedly.

"Do you hunt or shoot?" asked Poppet.

"I was brought up to do so, but I'm not a keen sportsman. And as for hunting these deer, I loathe it. I know they strip and destroy the trees, but the moor is big enough for them, I say.''

When lunch was over, Robin was left to rest in a sheltered nook. Muffet and Poppet explored the wooded coombes below, and Allister and Twinkles wandered off together. It was an ideal afternoon and one that lingered in their memories for many years.

''Oh,'' said Robin just before they started home, ''how I wish I could always live in the open air! I feel a different creature, my brain is brimming with thoughts, and every ache and pain has gone!''

''I believe we will make a cure of you, when we get you to Italy,'' said Allister. ''You want more sun, as I told you. Don't you think you'll see another winter here, for you won't! I'm returning, if all's well, the beginning of next September. The end of it will see you out with us in an unpretentious villa on the outskirts of Genoa. Twinkles won't hear of anything but a most prosaic and modern building. I am beginning to think I shall degenerate into a henpecked husband. She is turning me already from a jolly vagabond into a straightened automatic toiler. We shall settle down to a respectable dull——''

Twinkles put her hand lightly over his mouth. ''We shall do nothing of the sort! If your future seems so dull, go back to your jolly vagabond life, and leave me out of your calculation."

"Ah!" said Allister with a deep-drawn breath. "You have laid a spell upon me with your witchery. But I can break it with my fiddle."

"Will you come down to play to us one evening soon?" demanded Robin eagerly. "You don't mean seriously that you never play now?"

"Yes, you must come to-morrow night," said Twinkles. "And then we will see if your fiddle and I are rivals. Why, I love it as much as you do, and you know it!"

The ride home was as enjoyable as the time spent on the moor, for Allister took them back a different way, and every one of them—Robin included—were feeling much the better for their outing. As Poppet remarked in her slow, old-fashioned way:—

"It isn't waste of time to make oneself more fit for daily duties. A spring tonic is good for everyone, and we've had ours to-day!"

Yet they little knew what awaited them upon their return.

CHAPTER XVII.

WHAT THEY HEARD IN THE MOONLIGHT.

"Look!" cried Muffet suddenly from her front seat in the car which she was sharing with the chauffeur; "what is that red glow?"

"A fire!" exclaimed Allister; "and a fire in our village too!"

They were a couple of miles out of the village; but the sky was illumined by a bright red glow, and as they sped along a column of smoke was ascending and the scent of it reached them.

"Oh!" gasped Poppet. "It is either our house, or the post-office. How awful!"

And this proved indeed the case. A dense crowd was round the post-office, which was blazing fiercely; there was no lack of hands to cope with the fire. Buckets of water were being poured on the thatch, but as they came in sight a hoarse shout went up.

"Come back, you fools! 'Tis no use wastin' lives! Naught can save un!"

"Is Kate safe?" was Muffet's first cry. And then that good woman bustled forward directly she saw the motor. Allister was out at once, for Robin had breathed one anxious word, "My manuscripts!" and as yet Robin's room was safe and intact; it was the roof that was burning fiercely.

Twinkles and Muffet were impulsively dashing after him, but they were stopped by a farmer.

" 'Tisn't safe for you young ladies."

"But our things. We can bring something out. Oh, let us go. We must save something! Is there no fire engine?"

"The engine has been sent for, but these old cottages burn like tinder. We'll do our best, missy. But don't you venture nearer!"

The heat and smoke were blinding. Through the mist of it the girls watched men and boys dragging their bits of furniture out, Allister the busiest among them. They felt almost paralysed. Kate could do nothing but sob and bewail for herself. The fire had originated in her back parlour. An old lamp had been upset when lighted, and the little muslin curtains had caught fire at once.

Allister came towards them presently, and dumped down in the car beside Robin a large packet of his papers.

"Look here, this is not the place for any of you. Go up to the Hall at once. My mother will be delighted to put you up. We'll save all we can, but I'm afraid it won't be much. It isn't a pleasant sight. Don't stay here!"

"We must," cried Twinkles. "All our possessions in the world are in this cottage. It's awful. We must wait to see how much is saved!"

The others echoed her words. Allister went back, for he had no time for expostulation, and it was not very long before the roof fell in with an awful crash, and the flames shot up fiercely again into the sky. It was then that Muffet saw Robin's white strained face and Poppet's scared eyes. And she felt that a move would be wise.

"It's only torturing ourselves to watch," she said. "Let us come to the Hall."

"I won't leave Allister. He will be burnt next!" cried Twinkles, a little hysterically. "Leave me, Muffet. I am all right with Kate. I will come on afterwards."

And this they did. The chauffeur took them straight up to the Hall. Lady Eleanor was just in the act of sending down for them, for she had heard of their return. It was a tragical end to their day of pleasure, but as Muffet sensibly said:—

"We were mercifully kept out of harm's way, for if Robin had been left alone at home, he might not have been able to escape quick enough."

There was little or no sleep for them that night.

Twinkles returned with Allister about a

couple of hours later, having seen all of their possessions that had been rescued, safely stored in a friendly farmer's barn. Allister was covered with grime and smoke and had singed one of his hands rather badly.

"I don't believe one of our things would have been saved but for you," said Twinkles gratefully. She and Lady Eleanor were dressing his hand as best they could between them, in the library.

"I know what Somerset lads are," said Allister. "They use their eyes but not their hands in an emergency."

"Yes, they were just staring when we got up. I don't suppose more than half a dozen buckets of water were poured over our roof. But how awfully quickly the flames spread! I shall never forget the sight!"

Twinkles shuddered. She was quite unnerved, but she would not leave Allister until his hand was bandaged comfortably.

He bent over her tenderly.

"Good night, little woman. Go to sleep, and forget all about it for the time. The tragedy may prove a blessing in disguise."

But Twinkles shook her head. She could not see at present any light in such an awful catastrophe.

There was a grand consultation held the next morning amongst them all. Muffet was almost in tears.

"We shall never get another little cottage like it—never! We have made it so pretty! And now every bit of it is gone. We are absolutely homeless."

"I have a suggestion," said Lady Eleanor cheerfully. "The Dower House is empty. I was thinking of letting it. Why should you not be my tenants? It is furnished, but there is plenty of room for what you have saved."

Muffet looked up with shining eyes, then her face fell.

"We could not afford it. It would require so much to keep up; we should be obliged to have servants and they cost so much."

"Oh, I should let it with the servants in it. That would be my affair," said Lady Eleanor. "I want to have you nearer me. I want to know my future daughter-in-law better. And Colonel Blair has wanted Robin for a visitor again. You would be all close to us. Now think it over quietly. I am sure you will give me the pleasure of letting it to you."

"I don't know that your suggestion is altogether a good one," said Allister, who was pacing up and down the room restlessly. "I don't think they had better be settled down in a home of their own again. It has been taken from them perhaps to show them that it has served its purpose, but is wanted no longer.

"A home is waiting for Muffet in the Argentine. Poppet has one of her own choosing. And another home is waiting for both Robin and Twinkles in Italy. The sooner we all settle down in our respective homes the better."

Lady Eleanor smiled, but the girls looked perplexed and grave.

"What does Robin say?" she asked.

Robin looked up at her with a responding smile.

"I am willing to do just what is best," he said. "It is an awful shock to have our little home taken from us, but perhaps, as Allister says, it has served its purpose. God has given us so many friends that we ought not to complain. And I don't think I shall be a burden to any one, for now I am able to earn my own living."

He could not keep a touch of pride out of his tone.

Twinkles looked at Muffet and said nothing. It was a moment or two before she spoke.

"I had a letter yesterday from Gascoigne," she said. "He would very much like me to go out soon to him. He is lonely where he is and wants a wife to help him, he says. Of course I never meant to leave the Cottage for a year at least, but now I don't know—— What do you think of doing, Twinkles?"

"She thinks of coming out to me as soon as possible," said Allister promptly. "Her chief excuse hitherto has been that she could not break up the dear Cottage life. That excuse is swept away. I'll give her six weeks to make her arrangements, and then I'll ask you, mother, to bring her out, stay to our wedding, and wish us good luck!"

"And I shall be the only one left in England," said Poppet. "But I don't mind. I am perfectly happy where I am, and perhaps in my summer holiday I might manage to come out to Italy, Twinkles."

Twinkles did not speak; she seemed as if she could not. Allister looked at her in a very tender way, and then taking hold of her arm, he led her straight out into the garden with him.

"Now, sweetheart, don't look so sad! Tell me what is in your heart? Are you afraid to trust yourself to me? Don't talk of the Cottage, or the others, or even Robin, but talk of yourself. After all, it is your life and mine to be considered. Won't you come to me?"

When Allister pleaded gently, with all his soul in his eyes, Twinkles felt she could refuse him nothing. She looked up at him sweetly and seriously.

"Oh, Allister, you won't fail me! You are not really the irresponsible impulsive being you pretend to be? If you were, I should be afraid for our future. There are depths in you, I know; but I wish you would let me see them oftener. Life is not a game. I want you to help me to make the best of it, not waste our precious years in fluttering round and skimming the surface of things."

Allister drew her closely to him.

"I told you I was climbing, did I not? If I get a tumble you must help to pick me up. We'll climb together, my darling, and God above will help us both. Don't mind my chaffing. I never could—save to you—speak of things that lie closest to my heart. But I don't think I'll fail you. And as I told you, I know which is the happiest life for a man, an idle one or a laborious one, and I have made the choice, and I mean to stick to it."

"Then I'll come to you when you want me," Twinkles whispered.

And so Allister got his way.

But Lady Eleanor also got hers. She established them for the time being in the Dower House, and they made themselves very comfortable there. The girls determined to make their trousseaux themselves. Muffet gave up the post work, for Kate was so shaken in mind and body, that she announced her intention of retiring from the business, and going to live with a cousin of hers in the village. A fresh post-office was to be built, and a newly married couple were going to take possession; he was to be rural postman.

"All our struggles are coming to an end," Muffet said; "I can hardly get accustomed to lying in bed in the morning, till I am called. It seems such luxury."

"And I can hardly get accustomed to eating a meal which I have not cooked," said Twinkles. "But we shall have no time to be lazy."

And they had not. Poppet left them and returned to her situation, and Muffet and Twinkles sat and sewed together in the pretty morning room that had been formerly Lady Eleanor's special sanctum. Robin was in fairly good health, and in high spirits. He did most of his work out of doors, under a horse-chestnut tree on the lawn.

One afternoon Miss Walpole paid him a visit there.

"I have come out," she said in her quaint fashion, "to renew my youth. The sunshine of spring renews one's spirit, if it cannot do much towards one's poor old body. And a caretaker wants a strong spirit, eh, Mr. Author?"

"You have one," Robin said, smiling at her.

"It has a way of doubling up and collapsing," Miss Walpole said. "I assure you all this morning 'draughts' and the way to keep them off, a new pudding for dinner and the iniquities of two inefficient maids were quite sufficient to crush it. I even felt near tears at one time and then I came out; and nerves and heart and brain were braced and refreshed and strengthened. It's a pity I can't induce the General to get out more. He keeps his room to a temperature of 90 and finds the days unbearable. How is the writing getting on?"

"Pretty well. I nearly lost two month's work in the fire."

"What an awful visitation! I heard of it, and wanted to bring you all over to our place, but old people and young do not get on well together as a rule; and my brothers were not quite willing. Of course you are much better off here. It has all turned out for the best."

"Yes, even the fire!" said Robin; "though we did not think so at the time. We are breaking up our family circle, Miss Walpole. I don't half like it; but changes will come!"

"Ah, well," said Miss Walpole, nodding her head, "we all know that we shall see your sister Twinkles again. The village folk are already calling her the future Lady of the Manor. And she'll follow in the steps of dear Lady Eleanor. I have no doubt of that."

"Colonel Blair may get better and—and marry," said Robin. "I'm very fond of him, Miss Walpole; I hope he will live ever so many years yet."

"Perhaps he will."

Miss Walpole looked at Robin rather wistfully. "I hope you will grow stronger," she said; "there doesn't seem much of you to spare. I'd like to mention something to you. It's an old maid's secret, so you won't betray her confidence except to your sisters. I've left my bit of money to you. I made a fresh will the other day. I have no kith or kin belonging to me; and in the first instance I bequeathed all I had to the London Hospitals. But I fancy it may help you to write in comfort, and perhaps it will bring to your remembrance the poor old caretaker who goaded you on to better work than you were doing."

Robin was profoundly touched. He hardly knew what to say, and began to stammer out his thanks, but she stopped him.

"I don't want thanks. I only feel you will make a good use of what I shall need no longer. And it may relieve you from the danger of doing pot boilers. Good writing ought to be done with no eye to payment. You will never go back, will you?"

"I have vowed I will not," said Robin firmly. "I used to wonder when I was small, if my health would be good enough for me to be a parson, but it wasn't. And now I see that perhaps a pen may reach farther than a voice."

"To the uttermost parts of the earth," said Miss Walpole, fervently.

Robin's eyes glowed.

"You do me a lot of good, Miss Walpole."

She laughed in rather an embarrassed fashion. "I can't preach myself—never could, but there are many bits in a steam engine, and perhaps a small screw may be helping a great force along. Good bye, my dear boy. I can't stay long."

She was off. Robin lay still thinking.

"And if I'm conceited enough to compare myself to an engine, I am utterly useless without the real power—the steam. But that I can pray for, and it will be given."

Later on he told his sisters of Miss Walpole's promised legacy. Twinkles looked delighted.

"You are the most extraordinary boy for getting legacies!" she exclaimed. "Look at your old house! That would make quite a story in a book, and now this money! The Walpoles are very well off, though they live so plainly."

"But I hate the idea of her death bringing it to me," said Robin; "and I hope it won't come for ages. Perhaps when I lose my powers of thinking and writing, it will be a boon, so I am grateful to her. But that won't be yet, I hope."

"It will make you very independent," said

Twinkles thoughtfully, "but it will be better that you should be. Do you remember how forlorn and miserable we felt when Mr. Maxwell first told us that we were poor? We little thought how rich we should become in friends."

"Yes," put in Muffet, "and the hard work and frugal life has been very good for us. It has put grit and purpose into me, I know. I only used to think of enjoying myself at games before. And yet I have lived quite happily without them. I believe it would do everybody good to go through a year of poverty as we have."

"It has been a testing time," said Robin.

"It has taught me to cook," said Twinkles with her bright laugh. "They say if a woman isn't a good cook, she will never keep her husband contented."

Allister's last evening came. He spent most of his days at the Dower House, but Lady Eleanor insisted upon them all coming up to the Hall to dine upon this occasion. And after dinner, being a wonderfully warm night for the time of year, they wandered out upon the Terrace. Allister had always steadily refused to touch his violin; but Twinkles pleaded with him to give them a treat before he went.

He was with her alone when she made this request, and as he held her in his arms he looked down into her eyes with something of his old whimsical spirit.

"It shall be a serenade to you, my sweet."

"No, we will all enjoy it. Look! the moon is rising; let us come to the old sun dial and you shall charm our spirits there."

"My heart is breaking at our coming parting."

"It must be a very weak one to break at such a short parting as ours!"

"Ah, well, you'll see what my fiddle says! I will go and get him!"

In a short time they were all grouped round the sun dial. Colonel Blair did not join them, but Lady Eleanor was there. Allister's eyes were alight, as he tucked his violin under his chin.

"This is going to be its first and last appearance till I'm a married man," he said with a little nod at Twinkles. "After that you must bear the consequence if my music and my work clash together. Now I'm going to pour out my soul in thanksgiving. It has been starved. It is going to revel in a feast."

He stood in the moonlight, and after a little preliminary tuning he began to play.

His music was more wonderful than ever. There was a softer, tenderer strain in it than formerly, and it seemed to swell into something unearthly and sublime.

It spoke to each of his listeners in a different way. Lady Eleanor listened, and it took her back to the time when she held her boy in her arms, and prayed prayers, and dreamt dreams for his future. She had passed through waves of trouble and anxiety since; the music seemed to have a strain of that time in it, but it also spoke to her of peace after storm, rest after strife.

Poppet heard it, and saw spread out before her a vista of useful happy years; church bells and services; earnest eloquence in dim sanctified buildings; ministering visits to the sick and poor. Muffet listened with a smile playing about her lips. She saw before her the face and form of her handsome lover, a foreign country—but an English homestead; he and she the centre of a busy out-door life; and years of peace and plenty stretching out before them. Twinkles listened as under a spell. Her heart was throbbing still from his voice, his touch, his whispered words of love. Yet it was no serenade or love song he was uttering now. She was quick to distinguish that it was the portrayal of a soul's ascent from earthly aims to heavenly ones. And tears came to her eyes and great peace to her heart. Robin was in dreams of his own. Music always thrilled him through and through. "To suffer and be strong" chimed in and out, as the violin throbbed and swelled from pensive wistfulness and expectation, to ecstasy of fulfilment. But there was more than this. A time of test and trial, an opportunity for using a talent rightly or wrongly, and a burning desire to pass on to others some truths that however dimly comprehended at first would be seeds of a glorious harvest by and by. These were what the violin brought to him in the moonlight. And then, as the music vibrated with tremulous exultant joy, Robin's spirit leapt forwards to the time when he would be called by his King to hand back his heritage. He heard his mother's sweet voice again—"Rejoicing that they were counted worthy to suffer." And the light came to his eyes and a throb of joy was in his heart, as he murmured: "And not one of the weakest and smallest of them there would have changed their heritage for all the world; for had not the King given them the heritage of His Only Best Beloved Son."

As Allister became conscious of the rapt young faces about him, he knew that if his music had been laid aside for a time, his fuller and deeper experiences of life were making themselves felt with fresh power and force upon his beloved instrument now.

He played; and they listened and understood.